ARIELLA ISABELLA

Things I Almost Remember

A Bratva Romance

Contents

Content Warnings

This is a work of fiction. Names, characters, businesses, places, events and incidents are either the products of the author's imagination or used in a fictitious manner. Any resemblance to actual persons, living or dead, or events is purely coincidental.

This novel may contain :

- Assault
- Memory loss
- Homelessness
- Religious trauma
- Gun violence
- Gun violence against children off page (If you are familiar with the real Russian Romanov family, please remember that is will be a realistic depiction of their tragic deaths)
- Child deaths off page
- Gang/Mafia/Bratva activity
- Drug dealing / Gun dealing
- Mentions of past child abuse
- Violence
- Use of an unequal power dynamic
- Power play
- Mild Dom/Sub play where consent is always present
- Bondage / Blindfolds

- Drug Abuse / Alcohol Abuse / Addiction
- Mentions of past overdoses off page
- Blackmail
- Forced Marriage
- Mentions of pregnancy (No one gets pregnant)
- Threats of assault
- Threats of sexual assault
- Torture
- Violence between siblings
- One forced kiss between siblings
- Elements of racism
- Major Character Death

Dedication

This one goes out to the broken souls who want to punch destiny in
the dick.
Life is what you make it.

Glossary of Russian Slang

The below words and translation have been taken from police reports and article written specifically about Bratva language used with the United States. Many of the words will not translate directly.

Lisichka - Little Fox

malen'kaya ptichka - Little bird

zdravstvuy - hello

zhena - wife

niet - no

boltlivyy - mouthy

baklany - punks.

Sumasshedshaya shlyukha - crazy whore

Chto? - what?

milyy - dear

Vladyka - my lord or a way to address an orthodox priest

bandity - common word used among police referring to hoodlums.

blatnoi/blatnye - a catch-all term used by hoodlums to refer to themselves and their ('blatnoi';) way of life. The gangs' answer to police description of them as 'bandity.'

brat na pont - to bluff (take someone by storm).

bratski krug - circle of brothers; said to be main inner structure of vorovskoi mir; (also) 'bratskaya semyorka' (the brotherhood of seven).

brodyagi - a criminal caste below vor, vagabonds; (leaders-in-training).

byki - bodyguards; (literally bulls).

dan - taxes (tribute), collected by racketeers.

fartsovchik - black-market dealer, usually young, dealing in street-corner sales. Appeared in 1980s.

gastralyor - guest criminal (from other cities).

lavit kaif - to get high (on drugs), 'V. kaifu' means feeling pleasure at being high.

limoni/tri limona - nne lemon (million rubles)/three lemons (three million).

loshadka - in drug trade. Methadon (Russian word for little horse or hobby horse).

lunakhod - police van; literally moonwalker.

ment - cop.

mussor - cop; literally garbage.

na narakh - behind bars/in prison (zhoglo).

na svobodye - free from prison, 'in freedom.'

obshchak - criminal treasury.

patsani - young lads/warriors who make up criminal gangs.

pika - slang word for a knife. This is slang for the whole former Soviet Union.

po ponyatiyam - way of offering security services; gentlemen's agreement.

podkhod - coronation of vor; literally approach.

ponyal - understood

prishli mne kapustu - what you say if someone owes you money (send me the cabbage).

Ona bespolezna - She's useless

razboiniki - warriors of gang.

sborschiki - collectors who pick up taxes from traders at markets.

shalit - make mischief.

skhodka - criminal assembly/council of vory.

shpana - group of hoodlums.

suki - turncoats, scabs, traitors,; literally bitches.

tat - thief.

torpedo - contract killer.

tsekhovik/tsekhoviki - owner of black-market underground factories.

uryt - to kill; literally to bury.

vor - thief, lord of crime. Once generic term for thief or foreign enemy.

vorovskoe blago - criminal welfare. What every vor must defend.

vorovskoi mir - thieves world.

vzyat - to harass/rob; literally take, as in vzyat lariok (hit up a kiosk). Also means in slang, to take bribes.

zapodlo - shady business, underground commerce.

Ana

The streets of New York are said to be magical around the new year, with lights across every building and carolers on the street corners. The Hallmark movies always depict the areas you want to see, like Times Square or Rockefeller Center, with everyone with a smile and getting cocoa.

What a load of bullshit.

The winters on the East Coast can drop well below freezing, leaving much of the city's homeless population frozen to the sidewalk - and there are many of them. People funnelled out of stores with bags full of capitalist-driven bullshit that they would throw away before this time next year.

I held my thin coat close to my body as the December air made my teeth rattle, my fingers numb, and I looked almost blue. The high arches of the church were lit this time of night, a door that was always open to the desperate and cold. The Transfiguration of Our Lord is a church for lost souls and lower ranking bratva who stopped in only semi-regularly to pay respects to Father Grigori.

My hands pushed roughly against the large wooden doors, the wind helping me as my hair blew all around, and I struggled to close it behind me. After ensuring the latch was set, I moved further into the church and settled towards the back of the pews. There were only two other patrons here, the large clock near Father Grigori's offices reading just past one in the morning. But still, the doors were left unlocked, and the candles burned brightly.

I brought my fingers to my mouth and tried to breathe life back into them, the stale smell of cigarettes and grime making me wince. I hated smoking - I always have. But the nicotine chased away hunger, and the fire relieved my lungs from the cold. In the summer months, I'd stick to chewing gum and almost breaking the nasty habit, but then October would roll around, and so would a pack of Marlboros.

Crossing my arms, I leaned back against the hardwood, its comfort growing on me over the years. I'd grown up at Saint Basil's home for wayward children up the Hudson, so my ass had grown quite familiar with a pew. When I left there and came into the heart of the city, I made sure to find a good Russian church and plaster the biggest, *'I swear I'm not going to cause trouble'* smile onto my face in hopes of finding a safe place to rest my head. Father Grigori had seen right through it, but he didn't care. He was only concerned about my heritage and a promise to keep my drugs out of the church.

So far, I have managed to keep that promise until tonight.

My right hand absently patted my jacket pocket, the small bag of Oxycontin tucked away and ready to be sold for $50 a pop. I'd tried them once but threw up the contents of my stomach onto the dirty floor of a 7-11 not an hour later. Now, they were simply a job - an easy way to make half a grand in a night after my cut. It was my largest sale in one night.

I *almost* felt bad about passing the drugs off while in church, but there wasn't much else I could do after the orphanage kicked me out the doors on my eighteenth birthday.

What a sick excuse for a *home of God's children.*

I nervously looked over my shoulder to Father Grigori's office again, the lights were off, and I knew he'd gone home, but that didn't halt the race of anxiety I got from sitting here with this shit in my pocket.

Father had made me swear that I wouldn't come into the church with them, but I couldn't help it if my contact wanted to meet in a public place, and this was the only one I truly trusted.

Father Grigori had offered me a semblance of protection when I arrived. Others on the streets avoided hustling me for cash when they saw the cheap pendant of Saint Nicholas around my neck - Father Grigori's calling card.

My head swivelled when the large doors thudded behind me and let in another blast of cold air. The man who'd let it in was staring across the open floor and resting his eyes on the large painting of Saint Nicholas. The painting was spectacular, coated in gold, and over six feet tall. It must have cost the church a pretty penny.

Money that *could* have gone into the pockets of the community.

When his eyes moved again, they landed on me. He was an attractive enough man, maybe in his early twenties, and dressed far better than I. Likely a graduate student with spare change for a good time. I haven't the slightest clue what he'd do with over twenty pills - not my business, though.

He slid into the pew next to me, his knee bouncing uncontrollably while his head looked over his shoulder towards the closed office door.

Odd? Maybe he was orthodox.

I cleared my throat, his gaze swinging back to me with a dazed look. His eyes were bloodshot, and dark circles surrounded his whiskey-coloured irises. The man's jittery leg only intensified when I motioned for him to look forward.

"Lev?"

"Yep." He sighed and rubbed his nose with the palm of his hand.

A heavy user, by the looks of it.

"The money?" I wouldn't be the idiot handing over a grand worth of drugs if I didn't know the kid had it on him.

"Right. Right, sorry." He fumbled into his pocket and pulled out the cash, all in crisp *Benjamins*. Usually, drug users were forking over *Jacksons* and *Grants*.

I quickly snatched the wad of cash as I peered back at the still-dark office and then placed the pills into his side pocket. After ensuring no Father Grigori was hiding behind me in the pews, I stood to walk past him. I froze when his hand snapped out and latched around my wrist. "Wait," he said breathlessly.

"Let go asshole." I hissed at him. I looked around carefully again to make sure no one was watching us.

"*Svoyenravnyy rebenok?*" Wayward child.

It was a name for orphans in the orthodox church. The hairs on my neck stood straight up because a Russian buyer knew exactly whose territory I was in.

I nodded, snatching my wrist away from him and trying to leave, but he moved to follow me out.

"What's your name?"

I pulled the wooden doors open and slid out into the cold night, trying to make it around the corner before he saw me, but I heard his footsteps on the pavement.

"*Kak tebya zovut, dorogaya?*"

"It's improper etiquette to ask your dealer's name, Lev," I yelled over my shoulder while pushing into the night. The street lamps illuminated the gently falling snow, starkly contrasting the piles of trash along the streets. If I kept my head up, I could pretend this was a lovely night. But the man following me was trying to ruin that.

When his hand landed on my shoulder again, I spun around and snapped. "Hey! Piss off and take your candy back to your friends across town." I pushed him away from me, and his dark eyes were still wide - drug-fueled. "Or do yourself a favour, man, and go home. You don't need any more of that shit in your system."

He laughed. "Rich coming from a *gastralyor*."

I hunched my shoulders and sniffed, "I'm not an outsider; I grew up at Saint Basil's."

He reached into his pocket, took out a pack of cigarettes, and lit one. The grey plumes filled the space between us, and my mouth watered. "Then you're a *tat*. No one else is stupid enough to sell this close to Brighton Beach."

Lev was really starting to grate on my nerves, and the fact that he hadn't even offered me a drag was just a continuation of his bad manners.

"I'm not a thief either. You're the one that insisted on this area."

I knew what he was insinuating with Brighton Beach. It was the home of the New York bratva and the largest in North America. I usually circulated around Astoria, another Russian community with a church that would let me rest my tired eyes on cold nights. Still, this asshole had offered to buy my whole lot and requested Brooklyn.

I was now regretting it.

"Didn't think you'd do it, but it's worth a deal to not have and pay *dan* on top of street prices." He took another long drag from his cigarette, the glowing embers reflecting in his dark irises. He smiled happily, and I wanted to bash his head in - a new sense of anxiety creeping up my neck that had never been there.

"We're done here." I sneered while turning on my heel. The light glow of the street lamps no longer looked pretty, their brilliance now a trail back home as I wondered where to go for the night. I'd planned on circling back and sleeping at the church, but now I was more than willing to walk to the subway station and get the hell out of there.

"You're pretty. The *vor* won't be too upset, you know."

I tripped over my feet and the pile of garbage that lined the streets. I swung around and glared at his teasing smile, the cigarette still between his teeth.

"You got a *pika* under that coat, *milyy*?"

My hand went to my right pocket, where I usually kept my knife and froze when it was empty. My eyes grew wide as his smile spread. "Pretty, pretty *milyy*," he lifted his hand to show my red army knife reflecting off the lamp light. "What are we going to do with you?"

I ran.

My feet slapped on the pavement as snow fell around me in thick clumps, my eyes watering against it while trying to stay ahead of *Lev*. I could hear him behind me, his steps sounding loud and near, but I didn't dare look back.

Fuck!

I'd sold in Brighton only a handful of times - none of which happened inside the church. How stupid could I fucking be?

I rounded the corner near the subway but decided it would be signing my own death certificate. If there wasn't a train, I'd be stuck there. I'd have to out-pace him and pray the drugs in his system kept him slow. I took Bayard St, hoping to cut through the park and lose him there.

My lungs were burning, and I could feel myself growing slower. He was shouting behind me, but I pushed forward. I knew what the bratva would do to a woman they caught 'stealing' in their area. I might not be a rival gang, but that was even more dangerous at times. I had no family to call my own or claim protection to, and Father Grigori would surely disown me if he found out I was selling in the TOL.

It was just me.

The park was dark, the large swimming area and picnic benches flying by me as I wondered where I could go. If I ran all the way through, I could catch a train at Nassau station. I don't know if I could keep running, though. The cigarettes had ruined my once formidable lungs, the smoke breaking down years of dance and track training in just a few winters.

I looked over my shoulder once and blinked when I didn't see him. My feet slowed on the sidewalk as I turned around and searched through the darkness for his face, but instead, I only saw trees and a thin man hunched near a table.

My chest burned; no matter how hard I breathed, there was no relief for me, but I had to keep moving. I turned around to head towards the station and instead ran into a brick wall - or it felt like one. I fell backward onto the hard ground, my hands making contact with the pavement before my ass could. When I looked up, I saw the shadowed face of a man who was most definitely not Lev.

"Hey, are you alright?"

I looked behind me only to see an empty park, my body shaking from adrenaline before I looked back at the man. His black hair was shaved down short, though it fell into his dark eyes lit with worry. "Is someone after you?"

I forced a laugh out of my lungs. "Just an angry lover, nothing to worry about."

The man bent down and grabbed my arm, lifting me from the cold ground and pressing me to his chest. "A beautiful woman running through a park at one in the morning? I think that's a *little* concerning, don't you?"

His body was warm against mine, his arms like a cage around my shoulders as I tried to catch my breath. When I pulled away from him, he let me step back, but his eyes followed my every move.

"You're also in the park," I told him wearily.

The man smiled, his eyes feeling warm and inviting as he nodded. "I guess I am." He was obscenely handsome and maybe in his early thirties.

I raised a brow, and he continued. "I had a lot on my mind from work and needed to get my head on straight - the cold usually helps."

"Yeah," I agreed. "I'm trying to get to a subway station." I closed my arms around myself and peered around the empty park while the stranger raised a dark brow.

"I can walk you, of course, but do you have somewhere safe to go home to? If your scorned lover is out there -".

"He's harmless - just didn't take the breakup well. Do you mind having this conversation on the way to the subway?" I had already started walking out of the park as the man followed me.

As we exited on the opposite side of where Lev had chased me, I relaxed a little as my eyes landed on the handsome face of my savior. Odds are, the junkie had seen me bump into him and didn't want to involve anyone else.

"So, where's home?" He asked me while handing over a cigarette, which I graciously accepted between shaking fingers. I took the time to look over the man, his black coat pulled taunt over muscular shoulders and the leather band of a watch peeking out from under his sleeves.

He wasn't homeless.

"Sometimes Astoria, other times Brooklyn."

He nodded as he gave me a lighter. "And tonight?"

His eyes lit up playfully, and I couldn't help but smile. Okay, he was a beautiful man. His sharp features are somehow inviting and warm, while he also looked like he could have walked off a Calvin Klein magazine, and I wouldn't be the wiser.

"What's your name?"

The stranger's eyes twitched momentarily before he grinned. "My friends call me Leo, but you can call me whatever you like."

I threw back my head and laughed, smoke billowing from my mouth as Leo looked surprised. "You're pretty smooth, you know that?" There had been very few times that a man had surprised me, and it was always lovely to be taken by surprise when it was a welcome one. My handsome stranger was looking at me like I was a fine feast, and I was so cold that I considered letting him have a taste.

"I've been told once or twice. And what can I call you?"

I flicked the cigarette to the side and stopped in front of the stairs leading down into the rat-infested New York subway, the pale green fluorescent lights illuminating my apprehension. "Do you want to go get a coffee Leo?"

His eyes lit up at my suggestion, obviously surprised by my straight-forwardness. For a moment, I thought he'd kindly decline my offer, see me to the steps of the subway, and I'd be on my way. But then he smiled - a genuine and warm smile that made my chest ache as I offered me his elbow.

"It'd be my honor."

Ana

We settled into the back of a twenty-four-hour diner near the East River, a warm but chipped coffee mug between my frozen fingers as Leo stared at me like I had the answers to every question he'd ever dared ask himself.

"I never got your name." He was leaning back on his side of the booth, his right arm stretched over the well-worn cushion the colour of a sun-bleached stop sign.

"You didn't," I smirked into my coffee as he pursed his lips. He had a beautiful set of cushion lips.

"Well then, I'll have to name you myself."

My brow rose. "Oh? And what sort of name would fit a girl like me?" Leo continued to smirk at me as his eyes roamed over my body, reading for some hint as to what my given name might be but coming up empty-handed. There was simply nothing noticeable or striking about myself. I sat in a donated coat from the church, my red hair pulled back into a loose braid.

He assessed me for another moment before he grinned. *"I, however, after I had got into bed with Circe, besought her by her knees, and the goddess listened to what I had got to say."*

I smirked. *"And I will tell you of all the wicked witchcraft that Circe will try to practice upon you."*

Leo couldn't hide his shock. "You're a fan of Homer?"

"My schooling was thorough in classic literature - mythos not being excluded." If anything, the orphanage had directly moved *against* modern literature and culture.

His eyes darkened, lips tugging back over his pearly teeth that I imagined could leave beautiful marks on my skin. "So then I have to ask if you plan to ply me with potions and turn me into a swine or allow me to besought you with pleasure and pleasantries?"

My stomach flipped, knees pulling together under the table as warmth pooled between my thighs. Oh, this man had a wicked tongue, but I could be just as cruel.

"I can be swayed away from my potions, but I'll need more than coffee to allow Odysseus between my knees."

Leo nodded before slipping out of the booth and offering me his open palm. "Allow me."

I had been no stranger to one-night stands, the temporary heat from another's body to keep me warm in the darkest of winter months and supplied with alcohol in others. I had not been accustomed to the wealth in which Leo must have dripped and his fancy townhouse sitting in Cobble Hill. The brick home loomed over me like a deterrent, the million-dollar exterior screaming, *'You don't belong here!'*

"Are you coming?" Leo's voice broke through the negative thoughts in my mind as he called down to me from his front door.

I climbed the steps made for blue blood and felt the gaze of the neighbourhood at my back as I stepped through the front door and found myself in the most beautiful home I'd ever seen. The curling bannisters were dark in contrast to the light wood of the floors, and the moon cast a hazy light through a well-placed window above the entry.

"Your home is magnificent," I muttered mostly to myself.

Leo walked ahead of me into the home. His voice was muffled among the heavy tapestries that lined the walls and plush rugs below my dirty feet. "Inheritance can be both a burden and boon. Heating this place in the winter is much more of a curse."

Somehow, I doubted him and his nonchalant approach to such a domicile. Yes, family homes were more common among the upper class in New York, but there was hardly a sign that the wealth had fallen away. The paint was new, the furniture well polished, and the antique mirrors clear as day.

"But it did come with an impressive wine collection."

I tore my eyes away from the ornate furnishings as Leo came around the corner with a bottle of red wine that looked far too fancy for a quick fuck. I raised a brow. "Do you have vodka?"

Leo grinned, dropping his hand, holding the outlandish spirit, and backing down the hall again. "Do you have a preference?"

I shook my head.

When he was out of sight, I allowed my eyes and fixate on the woman in the mirror. She was the shell of something that had once been beautiful, much like the dilapidated homes of unwealthy kids who suffered under the weight of their parent's inheritance, of which Leo was not one. Her eyes were a bright blue, hidden below freckle sprays that lined her upper cheeks and nose. The red hair that was so half-heartily pulled back in plaits held the potential of so much more than it was being used for.

What was much more worrying about the woman was her gaunt cheeks and hollow eyes. The inevitability of homelessness wears down on fine breeding and a firm upbringing. She had once held so much potential, and now the memories of a life where it wasn't wasted on cheap alcohol and quick sex became more and more distant as the days passed.

The soft creak of a floorboard tore my eyes from the sad woman and back to the handsome stranger who held a bottle of Grey Goose in his strong hands. His dark eyes glanced between the reflection of the woman and myself. A shadow of worry danced across his features before disappearing behind his smile.

We sat beside a roaring fire in the front room of the monstrous Brooklyn home, the flickering light casting shadows into every corner as Leo passed me the bottom of liquid courage.

"So tell me, *Circe*, why did you and your scorned lover come to an end? Did your potions lose their potency?"

I rolled my eyes before taking a deep drink of the chilled alcohol that set my body alight. "It had simply run its course," I lied.

I couldn't tell him I'd been running from a Russian gang member who had set me up in an orthodox church where I sometimes slept because I was homeless. I doubt there was enough alcohol in the world for those words to escape my lips.

I looked sideways at Leo, who was leaning against the wooden table, our legs outstretched on the Persian rug that could have fed a family for years.

He hadn't even asked me to remove my soiled boots when I walked through the door.

"So you're not one for commitment?"

The question caught me off guard, and I winced. "I'm not opposed to commitment if that's what you're asking. But if I've ever found someone worthy of it - no. I haven't."

Not that I'd ever tried.

He took the bottle from my hand and set it on the floor between us. "A romantic then?"

"The more I know of the world, the more I am convinced that I shall never see a man whom I can love. I require so much!"

He smirked. *"Beware how you give your heart."*

"Only solidifying tonight's earlier events that inevitably lead me here. I'm not looking for love, Leo, just a good time." A warm body to be pressed against and another notch on my bedpost of shame and debauchery.

When I reached for the bottle of spirits again, his hand wrapped around my wrist and halted me. "Why settle for a good time when I promised you pleasure? I am a man of my word, after all."

I shivered.

His hands crept under the sleeve of my coat and gently ran across my naked wrist, his eyes sweeping my face for any sign of reluctance - there was none.

"Have you ever explored the boundaries of rapture, my sweet Circe? Felt the pinch of rope around your body and craved its burn?"

I couldn't speak, my head shaking slightly as my mouth went dry. Leo pulled firmly on my wrist, forcing my body towards him as his other hand tangled in my hair. "Do you want to burn with me, Circe? If only for a night?"

I nodded.

It was just a night; I'd had plenty of other one-night stands with far less attractive people.

Leo tutted. "I'm afraid you'll need to give your verbal consent if you want to play."

I swallowed. "Yes."

"Yes, what?"

"Yes, I want to play."

His lips crashed into mine before I could breathe, my mouth opening in shock, which allowed his tongue to push forward and take control. We tasted like vodka and coffee. Night and day. Pain and pleasure as he wrapped my braid around his palm and tugged my head back so he could stare down into my eyes.

"Don't you want to know the rules before you agree to play, witch-ling?"

I moaned, my fingers reached for him as he watched me struggle in his grasp. The fire had warmed the left side of my body; a flush heat swept across my cheeks as his mouth opened - tongue running across his bottom lip. "You're going to need a safe word to play with me. Are you familiar with that?"

I'd never had to use them; my sultry attempts at power playing never went very far with the men whose bed I warmed. Not that any had ever given me the confidence that they could fulfill the role of a dominant beyond rutting on top of me until they were spent. I'd read enough about them, though, their use and importance when engaging in sexual behavior that could otherwise turn harmful if you didn't tread lightly.

I tried to swallow, but the angle of my head made it nearly impossible, and it came out more of a groan. "Odyssey."

Leo smiled appreciatively before bringing his other hand up to cup my cheek. "Tonight, you're my goddess, and I am the traveler. I will not stop until the sun peaks through the windows of my home and your voice is raw from howls of pleasure. Are you ready to begin?"

Ana

I knelt in the middle of a large room, my bare knees digging into the carpet as Leo walked around me appreciatively. "You are beautiful, alluring, and too dangerous for your own good, Circe. I would think myself a fool to try anything with a witch who can see through my soul." He stopped in front of me, a satin blindfold in his hands. "Will you make this a fair fight, witch?"

He wanted to blindfold me, and I needed to trust him to do that. I should have walked out the front door at the thought of giving myself to this man without being able to see what he was doing, but something inside of me screamed for him. I begged the woman who controlled my mind to let me have him.

I nodded. "Yes."

"Yes, what?"

"Yes, sir."

He grinned, leaning forward and casting me into silky darkness that caressed my skin and chased away the dim lighting of his bedroom. I could feel his fingers linger around the base of my neck, his calloused hands dancing along the sensitive skin under my chin.

"I'm going to take off my belt, and I want you to pull my cock from my pants and hold it firmly. Can you do that, Circe?" His voice was like the darkest chocolate, rich and full of body that made me groan.

"Yes, sir."

His hands pulled away from me, and I could hear his belt come loose and fall to the floor, followed by what I thought was his shirt. I suddenly hated the blindfold, hiding what I assumed would be a perfect body fit for a god. When the fabric of his pants tickled the stray hairs that had lose from my braids, I raised my hands to run from his knees to the loops of his pants. My right hand palmed over his growing cock that was still held prisoner behind the fabric.

"Now, take it out and stroke it. Slowly."

My fingers dipped below the waistband of his boxers, brushing past his coarse hair until I had a firm grasp on the shaft of his cock. I used my other hand to pull his boxers and pants the rest of the way down so that I could get a good hold on him. When I wrapped my fingers tightly around his hardening cock, I heard a low growl from him. "Fuck"

He was incredibly hard and girthy, his cock being nearly too large for me to wrap my fingers around fully, and I wondered how he would ever fit. My mouth watered as his hips jerked forward, his warm length throbbing in my hand as I coaxed moans from his lips.

"That's a good girl, Circe. You look so perfect on your knees for me."

My legs spread below me, extending out so that my bare pussy was brushing the floor. I tried to move against it - to relieve some of the tension but his hand wrapped around the back of my head as he cursed. "Don't you fucking dare. Your pleasure belongs to me, and I'm not ready to give it to you yet. Open your mouth and stick out your tongue."

Without hesitation, my lips fell open, and I felt the head of his cock push lightly against my wanting tongue; the taste of his pre-cum was like an aphrodisiac that shot straight to my throbbing clit, and I moaned against him.

He took this as permission, pushing into my mouth slowly so that I could adjust to his size. The corners of my lips stung as I stretched around his cock, spit dripping down my chin as Leo showered me with praise.

"You're doing such a good job for me, witchling. You look so pretty with my cock in your mouth, and I bet you sound like a siren when you choke on it - begging me to take your breath away."

I nodded my head, sliding my tongue under his shaft and enjoying the way he felt in my mouth. His hand was still wrapped around my braid when he spoke. "We're going to start playing, Circe. I want you to take my whole cock until you can't breathe, and I'm going to hold you there until I think you've had enough. If you want me to stop, you'll need to tap on my hip twice. Like this," he said, guiding my hands to his hips. "Nod, if you understand."

With his cock still firmly between my lips, I raised my chin up and back down again.

"Good girl," he purred as his hand grasped my throat to hold me in place. I felt his hips push forward, his cock moving further into my open mouth as I held my breath. I couldn't see anything; the darkness around me forced all of my attention to the sensation of his warm, throbbing cock in my throat and the smell of his cologne as my nose brushed his pubic bone.

My hands were gripping onto either side of his hips as he rocked into my mouth, using me for his pleasure as my body shook with need. The feeling of his cock gliding through my lips, over my tongue, and down my tight throat made me moan - sending vibrations through him until he groaned.

"Your throat feels so fucking good while it's squeezing my cock, Circe. Your beautiful lips wrapped around me like a vice. Is your pussy the same beautiful, blushing shade of pink?"

I groaned, my hips involuntarily grinding against the floor as his fingers dug into my throat. I bet he could feel his cock through my skin, sliding into me as he used me for his own pleasure and fulfillment. The thought of being wanted - used for his cock made my body shake with delight.

When Leo pulled back until it was just the head of his penis in my mouth, I allowed myself to take a deep breath while my tongue wrapped around the sensitive underside of the head.

His hand caressed my hair as I moaned. "Please."

I'd never begged for cock in my entire life, but here I was on the floor of a beautiful stranger's home with a cock between my lips and a need so great between my thighs that I wanted to cry.

"You did such a good job taking my cock. Do you think a reward is in order?"

I nodded. "Yes. Yes, sir."

His hands wrapped under my arms and helped me to my feet. A dull ache in my legs made me want to sit back down, but he started walking me across the room until he turned me and pushed me back against a bed so that my legs hung off. His fingers wrapped around my wrist, and I felt a thin piece of fabric tie my hands together until he pushed them above my head.

"I'm going to reward you for taking my cock like a good girl, but if you move, then you're going to be punished. Understood?"

"Yes, sir."

Leo got down in front of me, his breath on my bare pussy as I struggled not to move. Being blind to everything he was doing amplified his skin on mine - his lips on my inner thigh. "Hmm," he moaned. "The same blushing shade of pretty pink for a pretty pussy."

I sucked in a breath as his trailed feather-light kisses from my knee up my thigh until his tongue darted out to flick my swollen clit.

My back lurched off the bed when he touched me, and I yelped when his hand swiped down and slapped my center. "That will be your only warning, beautiful."

I settled myself back on the bed as Leo's fingers dug into my thighs and opened them wider. "You are a sight to behold, my darling witch."

This time, when his tongue flicked across my sensitive skin, I bit into my bottom lip and shuddered internally. His mouth was on me in an instant, warm and controlling, as he pushed and prodded me toward the end of oblivion. I'd never had a man venture between my thighs like this, soft curls brushing my legs and stubble from his cheeks rubbing at my skin. It forced me to the end of a cliff, and then he backed away.

I whimpered, my arms on either side of my ears - bound - and my eyes still cast in darkness so that *he* was my only sensation. His fingers massaged my legs, pushing them open further until I was spread out further than I ever thought possible. My many years in ballet were to thank for the view Leo was surely getting of me.

I opened my mouth to beg him - cry out for him to put his mouth on me again, but then I felt him stand and lean over the bed. "My darling witch, I'm going to fuck you now. I want you to move and scream as you please but do not come until I give you permission. Do you understand?"

My body shook, chills running down my spine as my hips rocked against the air in a wanton motion. "Please, sir. Please fuck me."

Without hesitation, he jerked his hips forward and speared me on his cock, my body shuddering at the sudden intrusion and size of him. "Fuck, Circe. Your cunt is even tighter than your throat."

"Oh, God!"

He laughed. "No, he's not the one fucking you right now. I am."

Leo's hips slammed into mine at a back-breaking pace, his moans loud in my ear as he fucked me mercilessly. I could feel his sweaty body gliding over mine, his rock-hard abs pressed tightly to me as I climbed higher and higher toward Nirvana.

With every thrust, another one of my walls fell. With every moan, my body shivered in delight and need. While Leo was fucking me, using me, and bringing me to the edge of pleasure - I was simultaneously letting him. Giving him control over my body and trusting this stranger to bring me peace. Quiet the world around me and make me focus on the now.

As his finger brushed against my clit, I took in a deep breath. My legs were shaking below us as Leo forced pleasure onto me, and I willingly allowed him to. He was in charge, but only because I let him be. It was intoxicating. Erotic in the most profound meaning of the word. His thumb made lazy circles around the sensitive area between my thighs as he continued to fuck me, and without thinking, I allowed myself to creep towards the edge of that cliff.

The sound of our bodies danced around the room, his moans forcing me closer to the edge even as part of me knew I wasn't allowed to. But I didn't care.

With a shudder, my body came around his cock, and I screamed into the void. The darkness around me welcomed the pleasure, basking in it and settling like a deep pool - until a low growl pulled me from that temporary bliss.

"I told you not to come until you were given permission, and now my cock is squeezed like a vice grip by your tight pussy. You're going to have to be punished, my wicked witch."

"I'm sorry." I whimpered.

"No, Circe, don't lie to me. You're not sorry in the slightest. No, I bet you're actually looking *forward* to your punishment."

I groaned, my hips rocking forward on his cock before his hands latched onto me and held me down. "You are a filthy fucking witch, aren't you? You took everything my cock could give you, and now you want more. What am I going to do about that, Circe?"

I pulled my bottom lip between my teeth before I spoke. "Punish me, sir. I've misbehaved, and now I need you to punish me."

He groaned. "You're so perfect, little witch. Little goddess of mine. Even when you misbehave, I can't help but want and feel you come around my cock again. But you have to be punished, sweet witchling. Filthy fucking goddess."

"Please," I cried around as he pulled out of me. The sudden feeling of being empty of his cock made me want to scream and beg for him. He stretched me so perfectly, his hips fitting with mine like a missing piece of myself.

I couldn't see Leo, but I could hear him walking around the other side of the bed where my head was as I wiggled on the duvet. When his hands grasped my arms and pulled me forward, I had an idea of what he wanted. He put my tied hands in my lap while my head fell backward off of the bed.

"I'm going to fuck your throat now, and it will be deep and for my pleasure alone. I don't want to hear your moans right now - this is supposed to be a punishment, Circe. Do you understand?"

"Yes, sir. A punishment."

His hands gently caressed my cheek. "Good girl. Now open your mouth."

I did as I was told and relaxed when his cock settled on my lips, the tangy sweetness of my orgasm still slinging to his cock. My tongue sticking out so that the top of his cock glided into my mouth with ease. Leo's hands wrapped gently around my throat as he held me in place. "Your tight little throat was made for my cock, you wicked thing. I could get used to fucking your face like this."

I wanted to moan my response, but I stayed quiet per Leo's directions as he started to thrust into my mouth. His cock pushed further between my lips as Leo took his pleasure from me, using me to reach his climax like the filthy little goddess he made me feel like. As he forced his way into the back of my throat, I gagged, and my body lurched forward only to be held in place by his firm grip. "No, you have to lay there like the filthy fuck toy that you are. This is your punishment for coming without permission, Circe. You're going to take my cock, and you're going to be quiet about it."

I should have felt ashamed and disgusted with the way he spoke to me, but instead, I felt my pleasure soaking the sheets between my thighs. Laying here in this stranger's room, completely at his mercy as he used my throat as his toy, was the most feminine and powerful I'd ever been in my whole life. Leo's hips shuddered, slamming into my face as his calloused hands moved toward my breasts and squeezed my pebbled nipples. "So fucking perfect."

When he lurched forward, his throbbing cock releasing his cum down my throat, he moaned into the night. "Fuck. Fuck, darling. Oh, my wicked little goddess. You filthy fucking witch." And when his fingers twirled my nipples hard, he moaned, "Come for me."

And I did.

Ana

My body ached, legs and arms feeling heavy as I stretched out across a soft linen bed. I hadn't felt this exercised since I was a girl, dancing to Stravinsky and Tchaikovsky in front of an empty auditorium. The orphanage had instilled discipline in us through exercise, using ballet to control the body and wither down the spirit - though the seats were always empty.

Who would ever show up to watch orphans dance?

I'd been dropped off at the doors of St. Basil's when I was a young girl with nothing but the clothes on my back and the faintest memory of a woman with auburn hair and a gold pendant around her neck. Every year, those memories became more clouded - dream-like.

I could sometimes close my eyes and try to create her face in my mind, but now it was something I could almost remember. Just out of reach - much like many other dreams I had when my lashes fluttered shut. How could nearly a decade of life disappear? There were things I could almost remember, like the smell of mulled wine and burning sparklers, but then I'd close my eyes, and it'd all turn black.

I raised my arm over my head and sighed, my fingers twitching for a cigarette and my legs straining against the sheets that had cocooned me. I could barely tell that there was a madman beside me; the soft exhale of his breath was the only tell-tell sign that I wasn't dreaming again.

Opening my eyes, I stared up at the ornate ceiling of his family home; doubt still riddled me, though. What did it matter if he was rich anyway? This wouldn't happen again, so our two very different social classes didn't matter. I got a night of bliss, and he got off.

Everyone wins.

But when I turned my head to look at the stranger who'd wooed me into his bed, my heart stopped. Etched into the tan skin of Leo the Stranger were dark Russian tattoos. Tattoos that I had been unable to see last night because I was blindfolded and fucked to exhaustion.

Bratva tattoos.

I sat up, my palm digging into my eyes as if I could chase away what I was seeing, but no - there was most definitely an Orthodox Cathedral in the center of his muscular back and an *S* on the back of his neck.

Fuck.

I slowly lifted the covers from my sore legs, twisting sideways and sliding away from him as I continued to watch his breathing. He seemed asleep, but I wouldn't risk being caught as I fled.

I gathered my clothes off his floor, stepping over the discarded blindfold and pausing when I noticed that there was still a shot of vodka left in the bottle. The sun was peaking through the heavy curtains in Leo's room, illuminating a habitual need inside me to feel numb. I downed the substance in one swallow before setting the bottle back down on the decorative carpet I'd dug my knees into the night before.

As I closed the door behind me, Leo still looked dead to the world, and I had to wonder what the odds were of running from the Russian mob just to run into the arms of another. He'd stepped out of the shadows last night like a dark knight, chasing away the consequences of my shitty actions. When he'd shown an interest in me, it didn't seem like a bad idea to enjoy the turn of events.

But that died when I opened the front door to stare into a pair of dark, bloodshot eyes.

"Hello, *milyy*."

I tried slamming the door shut, but his hands slipped into the crack, his body forcing the wooden barrier open slowly as he *tsked*. "Where's your hospitality, milyy? Won't you offer me a cup of tea?"

I released the door and barreled down the long hallway that I knew led to the kitchen, morning sunshine cascading off the stainless steel appliances and blinding me. I'd almost reached the back door when his hand latched onto my wrist and spun me around.

"You're already caught, little bird. Your flapping will only wear you down."

"Fuck you." I spat into his face and watched his eyes darken even more. Lev's features looked much older in the daylight, and it was so obvious now that he wasn't a college boy looking for party drugs. Below the collar of his jacket, I could see dark ink that licked at his neck and disappeared into what I assumed was a cathedral, matching the one Leo had on his own back.

"You little *suka*," he sneered down at me as he pinned my arms to the side. "You smell like a bar. Take a little sip before trying to dash?"

Lev looked at me with a smirk and knowing in his eyes. An addict could always sniff another addict out, and here we were with his red eyes and my rancid breath.

"Did you take that bag back to your buddies or snort half of it before walking in the door? I think you missed a little . . ." I said while wiggling my nose.

He cocked his head and laughed, but it was drowned out by the sound of footsteps coming down the hall. I couldn't see a damn thing while Lev had me caged in his arms, but I could tell when Leo stepped into the room because the temperature almost dropped.

"Remove your hands from our guest, brother." He said it in such a bored tone as if it was trivial to find Lev in his kitchen with a girl captured in his arms.

I swallowed.

Lev looked down at me and smiled. "I told you the *vor* wouldn't mind with such a pretty face like that."

He released me, and I took the time to take three significant steps away from him so that my back was to the French doors and my eyes were trained on the two predators in the room. Leo wore a low-hanging pair of pajama pants, his dark hair tousled from sleep, and an open-face cardigan lazily thrown over his broad shoulders.

"You weren't going to say goodbye?"

He stood beside Lev, and I swore at myself for not seeing the astonishing similarities. Both men have dark brown eyes matching their hair and olive skin, which could seem alluring until you notice the bratva tattoos that mark them. Each man stood over six feet, Leo being the broader of the two, while Lev had a thinner frame.

They were almost twins and devilishly handsome.

"You weren't going to let me leave, were you? This was all a setup from the start." As the man smirked, I bounced from one foot to the other, but Leo looked far more relaxed than his brother.

It made sense now how a man like Leo would take someone like me home. It wasn't because he desired me - it was a trap with benefits, and I'd played right into their hands.

"It was a setup to have you sell in the TOL, but I never imagined you could outrun my brother. It seems he hasn't been caring for his health much lately." His eyes darkened towards Lev, who looked at the floor.

"What about fucking me? Was that a part of the plan, or was I prettier than expected?"

Leo's brows rose, but it was Lev who spoke. "Well, with a filthy mouth like that, who could resist?"

His brother went rigid beside him but didn't say a word as they stared me down like a meal. I had run from the dog just to be caught by a wolf - his jaws tightening around me so deliciously that I hadn't even minded.

Leo nodded towards the breakfast bar. "Take a seat."

"I'd rather this be quick."

He rolled his eyes and shared a look with his brother.

"All this because of a couple of pills? I would have thought that was small fish to men like you."

Lev went to open his mouth, a snarky comeback likely at the tip of his tongue, but Leo interjected. "Would your saintly Father Grigori think the same? I hear he has few rules for those who follow him - and you've broken his most sacred one."

There is no business on church grounds.

They knew I had been selling in their territory, so they devised a trap. A snare for an unsuspecting and desperate animal such as myself. "What do you want?"

Leo looked at me momentarily before turning on his heel and walking towards the shining espresso maker atop his granite counters. He seemed far too calm, collected, and in control for my liking, but I *was* in his control. I'd been caught red-handed, and by the laws of the church, I no longer fell under their protection.

"Do you know much about the organization you meant to undermine, *Circe*?" His dark eyes flickered to me as the machine in front of him started to fill the silence in the room.

My brows rose as I crossed my arms. "I only know *of* them. They're controlled by a family with much of New York in their pockets, and sometimes a face or two pops up in the TOL, but that's it." I'd made sure to stay clear of them whenever possible, and that's why I usually stuck to the dirty walls of Astoria rather than Brooklyn. Desperation had pushed me out of my den and forced me to look elsewhere for work - the job outlooks in the small Russian neighborhood for a woman like me had become increasingly *carnal*.

Leo set a small espresso cup that was now filled on the counter and started to make another. "The Solkovs control everything from the Hudson to Brighton Beach - hard won over a decade ago from the previous ruling family."

I snorted. "You say it like you're royalty."

"As close as you can get to it in New York," muttered Lev as he sat at the ornate breakfast nook. I looked his way as the white of his eyes continued to be swallowed by bright veins of crimson. I thanked the Lord I had never developed much of an appetite for narcotics.

Leo slammed the palm into the counter. "As I was saying, the Solkov Bratva runs New York and controls everything that comes to port with the help of a few other families. This control was gained through what many would consider a civil war with the tyrants being killed or driven from the city."

I snorted. *Tyrants* - like the bratva could be anything but. I looked between the brothers as Leo set a second cup of espresso on the counter and pushed it my way. "Drink."

I thought about arguing with him, but the bitter aroma entranced me. I hadn't had a good cup of espresso in who knows how long, and I hadn't gotten much sleep the night before, either. I raised the cup to my lips and tried, though miserably, to hold back the moan of pleasure as the coffee touched my tongue.

"Good girl," he said huskily.

I frowned at him as Lev snickered, and it heated my blood. I could see every ripping muscle of his chest and abdomen and remember how it felt below my fingers just hours ago. "This has been a fine story, but what do you want from me? If it's the money, then you can fucking have it."

Leo's dark eyes were alight with humor. "Such a mouth on you."

I snapped. "You weren't complaining last night."

Both men chuckled as Leo leaned across the counter, his eyes level with mine. "What I want from you and what I need from you are two entirely different paths, I'm afraid, *Ana*." His lips curled into a viscous smile that tore through me like a knife.

I swallowed. "No longer the witchling then?"

"Oh, I doubt you could ever stop, but I need the Ana that attended St. Basil's. *Circe* will have to stay tied away for now, though I doubt she minds the burn of the rope."

I shivered and immediately hated myself. It had been far too easy to run into his trap - leap into it willingly.

I straightened my back and attempted to seem collected, though, on the inside, I was a deep pool of anxiety and fear. "Well then, what can Ana do for you?"

Leo straightened and took a quick sip from his cup of espresso, eyes trained on me the entire time. "What can you remember from before your time at the orphanage?"

I took a breath and shook my head slightly. "Not much - maybe bits and pieces of a woman I think is my mother, but that's all."

"And what *about* this woman, do you recall?"

I huffed, annoyed. "I don't know. She had red hair and a golden pendant. I think I can recall the smell of vanilla and maybe her laugh." I shook my head as emotions welled in my chest. "Why?"

Leo looked over my head to his brother, a wordless exchange that left the room nearly silent. When he looked back at me, his lips curled. "I want to make you an offer, Ana. And before you say no, I want you to consider the situation you've put yourself in."

"You set. Me. Up." I growled at him.

His face dropped, shoulders flexing outwards as he stared down at me. "Don't act like you haven't been peddling in Brooklyn for over a year now - and we've *let* it slide."

"So what changed?"

Leo frowned; his gaze was penetrating, searing through me until I was exposed to him. "War."

Ana

I stared in bewilderment between the two men as their faces grew grim. "War? What war?"

"I told you that Vlad Solkov took New York by force, starting a civil war that drove the other families either out of town or into a grave. My father had thought himself on top of the world after he was crowned in front of the brotherhood as the ruling vor of the city and much of the state."

My hand grasped the new empty espresso mug, latching on the phantom warmth it provided my shaking hands.

"Like a dutiful usurper, he vowed that the heirs to the Romanov bratva were dead. For a while, he thought he had succeeded, but it turned out that a few people who worked for him had a problem with disposing of the youngest children. Alexei Romanov popped up in Chicago two years ago, now a man, and at the time, he seemed content with the windy city."

Lev stood and crossed the room, his hand outstretched with his phone. "We now know that this is not the case," he said as I looked down and gasped in horror. A picture of six headless men, bound by their hands, was being shown to me. Their bodies were lined up in an execution-style, Armani suits drenched in blood.

I gagged, "What the fuck?"

Leo pushed the phone aside and brought my attention back to him.

"Six of my men, for the six Romanovs that were thought to have been killed during the rebellion. His mother, father, and supposed four sisters - but he won't stop there."

I shook my head as if it could dislodge the image from my mind. "What does this have to do with me?"

Lev shuffled beside me, but Leo and I had our eyes locked. His dark hair was pushed back, a strand falling across his brows, and my fingers itched to push it back. "Unlike my father, I want to prevent a war that would leave this city in shambles. I have a responsibility to the people here, which means putting my neck on the line to keep Alexei out of the city."

"And me being from St. Basil's has something to do with this?"

"They never found all of their bodies," Lev said as he leaned against the bar. "There were plenty of witnesses who claim they saw the family dead, but no one has a grave site, and now Alexei is causing havoc - clearly alive."

He reached into his jacket and pulled out an envelope, his signet ring gleaming in the morning light as he pushed it towards me. Lev might have looked like his brother, but as the man twitched and rolled his shoulders, I couldn't help but pity the hole he'd fallen into.

Though I'd still like to see him fall into an early grave.

I grabbed the folder and opened it, struck again with images that moved me. The first was of a handsome man standing tall and proud, his hand placed gently on the shoulder of a small boy wearing the same dapper suit. Neither of them smiled, but the boy seemed proud rather than sad - stoic with his chin jutted out and head held high like his father.

"Alexei," I muttered. His hair was blonde and carefully styled, and his crystal blue eyes staring down at the camera like a dare. He couldn't have been more than ten years old.

The following photo was of four girls in matching white dresses, all lined up from oldest to youngest and posed in front of a grand fireplace strung with garland. The girls all looked similar, but while three favored the looks of Alexei and presumably their father, the most petite girl stood out. She was maybe six in this photo; her auburn hair was pulled back, and her thin face tilted down as her wide eyes glanced off to something in the distance.

"Anastasia Romanov," Leo's voice sliced through the silence. I looked up at him and saw that both brothers were studying me - watching my face for some reaction.

"The youngest children were spared," I muttered.

Both men nodded.

The last photo startled me like a phantom staring back through an open doorway. It was of a woman, her head tilted forward as her sky-like eyes pierced through the image and captured you. She had the same thin face as the youngest daughter; red hair swept over one shoulder and a finger raised to her chin in a knowing look.

I could almost hear her - imagine how she would sound when captured by humor and laughing as if no one else could hear.

My hands began to shake while captured in a trance by the woman - unable to look away from her eyes. I failed to think of anything but the smell of vanilla and gentle fingers under my chin.

A ghostly touch.

My body suddenly broke free, my chest heaving as I threw the photos onto the counter and forced back tears. "What the fuck is all of this?" Part of me knew what they were trying to tell me, but I didn't want to imagine it - I needed to hear it. I couldn't trust my thoughts very often, and I could still wake up on a park bench somewhere like this. It was a dream.

A nightmare.

Leo's face was blank of all emotions, his dark eyes trying to convey a truth I *needed* to hear.

"Say it. Out loud."

"We don't know for certain," Lev interjected, but Leo quickly held up his hand to silence him.

The dark-haired beauty - my Odysseus and strange traveler braced his hands on the counter and calmly spoke. "You arrived at St. Basil's just after midnight on New Year's Eve, the same year the rebellion happened. You had experienced a blunt force trauma to the head, and the doctors diagnosed you with a severe concussion - near total memory loss."

"I know all of that," I snapped. "But what are you suggesting? Are you saying that I'm some lost *bratva* princess? That's absurd."

Lev spoke up. "Only a DNA test can confirm it, but we've done the research. You're an heir - Anastasia Nikolaevna Romanov."

"Fuck off," I spit as a treacherous tear spilled from my eye. How dare they throw a family at me just for me to also find out that they're gone. Dead.

Leo stepped around the counter and stood before me; his eyes cast downward as I refused to meet his gaze. I felt trapped, lied to, and manipulated into something that I didn't truly understand. I felt his hand reach out and gently tilt my chin towards him, and I closed my eyes.

"I know this a lot -."

"How dare you," I snarled, tearing away from his grip. The brothers stood opposite of me with a mixture of concern and impatience laced on their faces.

"Who do you think you are to drop something like this on me? Are you here to finish the job?" Adrenaline spiked in my blood as their words played out. *Like a dutiful usurper, he vowed that the heirs to the Romanov bratva were dead.* Alexei causes chaos for them in Chicago, and now they want to tie up the loose ends.

Leo took a deep breath, his hands balling into fists at his side as he spoke to his brother. "This isn't going to work."

"You don't have another option," Lev sighed.

"I could put a fucking bullet between his eyes."

"No!" It was my voice that silenced the two. I had stepped towards them, my hands raised as if I could physically push the thought from their minds. "Don't kill him."

Lev snickered, but Leo's brow raised as he clenched his jaws. "You didn't even know you had a family a minute ago, and now you wish to bargain for his life?"

I swallowed, my eyes flickering to the photo of him and my dead father, whose name I'd never remember. "I have nothing to bargain with, but I beg you. Don't kill him."

Don't kill the little brother I never knew I had—the only family out there who could fill the gaps in my mind.

"You brought me here for a reason." I looked to Leo, who nodded his head. "Why am I here?"

"Alexei has made it very clear that he wants his father's throne back, but you have to understand that I am not willing to hand out New York to a young man who beheads my men before even reaching out to me. He has his blood for your parents and sisters, but he will never have New York. To make matters worse, the families of the men have sent bleeding crosses with Alexei's name on them." Leo said as Lev threw six papers onto the counters atop Alexei's photo. Each was on a ripped-out page of the orthodox bible; a red cross angrily painted atop the holy words.

"So, what does that mean?" I asked.

"It means, *milyy*, that your brother has a price on his head and there's only two paths a vor can take to wash away the debt owed. He either delivers Alexei's dead body to the families, or he makes him untouchable by *bratskaya semyorka* law."

"Okay," I shook my head. "How?"

Leo straightened, his broad shoulders tensing as emotions drained from his sharp features. The man I had gone home with and had shown me a night of unmatched pleasure was not the same man who stood before me today. "I join the houses, making Alexei my brother. By marriage."

My mouth fell open as I blinked at him, dumbfounded by the lack of humor on his face. "You're messing with me," I huffed. Lev shook his head as his jittery hand pushed through dark locks, and he muttered under his breath. "Why the fuck did I suggest this?"

My eyes snapped to him as a snarl escaped my lips. "You think this is all a joke? That my pathetic fucking life is a game to you *bratva* pigs?" Lev's eyes pinched in anger, but Leo continued to look unmoved - emotionless. "You're fucking crazy if you think I'd marry you."

Lev opened his mouth, but Leo finally spoke up. "You wouldn't be marrying him. You'd be marrying the youngest *vor* in the *bratskaya semyorka* and head of the Solkov family. You would be Mrs. Leonid Solkov neé Romanov - *my* wife."

Wife.

How foreign the word sounded to my ears - even more than a name I didn't recognize as my own. The men in front of me were everything that the orphanage and Father Grigori warned me to stay away from, and yet I had fallen right into their hands anyway. I might not have perished by the Solkov hand the night my family was killed, but here he was now. Leo Solkov, strange traveler and son to the man who ordered my family's murder. Holding my brother's life in his hands, and all I had to do to save him was give up my own.

"How do you know it will even work."

Leo grunted. "What do you mean?"

"What keeps Alexei from destroying New York anyway? He might be my brother by blood, but he doesn't know me. Would he stop his crusade for a woman who can't remember him?" I asked incredulously.

Leo smiled briefly before it fell from his hard mouth. "You were very quick to beg for his life - I'm hoping he will be the same."

I reared back in realization. "This isn't a way to save Alexei but another way to keep him submissive. If Alexei takes one step out of line, my life will be threatened. I'm just leverage."

"You're learning," Lev said.

I glared. "The big, bad Solkovs are scared of one man? Why wouldn't you kill Alexei if you're as powerful as your claim?"

"You asked me not to."

"I'm not that important."

Leo finally snapped. "Or I could kill you now and send your head in a box to your little brother!" He threw his hands into the air with annoyance. "It'd save me the hassle of keeping such an insufferable wife."

"Then do it! Fucking finish the job your father failed to do and save us both the misery of a marriage neither of us want!" I stepped forward and tried to push past Leo, but Lev reached out and grabbed my arm.

I spun around on him like a cornered animal and slapped him across his beautiful face - his eyes turning dark and dangerous as my chest heaved. "Get your fucking hands off of me."

"So my brother's hands were okay last night, but mine aren't worthy of you, princess?"

I glared into his dark eyes. "I wonder if I dropped a bag of pills if you'd dive like a dog at my feet?"

His wicked smile broadened, and his fingers dug painfully into my upper arm. "And I wonder how long you'd last without your liquid courage?"

"Enough!" Leo's voice cut between us as his hands tore us apart. He roughly shoved Lev aside and stepped closer to me so he could look down his nose at the ruined daughter.

"If you want to save your brother, you'll do as I say, and let me handle him. Once the ring is on your finger, there's nothing the brotherhood can do - but every minute you wait arguing like a brat is another minute that the seven families hunt for him. It's your choice, *Circe.*"

I was fuming, caught in a trap between a house fire and eternal damnation. I could either walk away and watch my brother be hunted like a dog - lost before I could ever find him. Or I could give away my autonomy—something I had held so sacred since leaving the orphanage.

I didn't know what marriage with a man like Leo even meant. I had seen movies about mob wives and the deadly occupation of their other half, but I never imagined myself in this situation—a sickly-looking orphan from New York handed chains made out of gold.

I lifted my chin and forced a sickly sweet smile onto my face. "When's the wedding?"

Ana

I stood in the center of an extensive library with dark, curling wood grain and floor-to-ceiling shelves. In the center of the room was a fireplace with a mantle well above my head and plush couches surrounding the hearth. It could have been out of someone's fairy tale, but now it was but a room in my nightmare.

Leo had abandoned me here on his way out the door without a backward glance, leaving me to explore his home and widdle out a corner to hide in. He said the wedding would occur within the week, and my fate would be sealed before the church. I couldn't help but think of my lost little brother who was out there with a thirst for blood and felt such utter sadness. I didn't have an easy life in the orphanage, but to grow up knowing what you'd lost? That must be the most painful childhood.

I slid across the room and gazed over the back terrace, now covered in snow, the dark gray skies promising that even more of it was on the way. My fingers brushed the crushed, green velvet curtains pulled back over the antique glass, and I smiled against my better judgment. I'd never been in a place like this.

I'd spent my youth trying to hide on a stage, spotlights following my every move and exposing me. I'd danced, twirled, and leaped out of my skin and into the costume of another, but it was no use. I would be incapable of breaking the chains around my memories. But here in this home, ornate fixtures and old photos of a family long gone made me feel even *worse.*

There would be no hiding here.

I could always run away - catch a train with some pocketed silver candle sticks and go god knows where. But what would happen to Alexei? To a boy - man - who'd ever known revenge? I couldn't help but taste his anger like a bitter drink that tried to drown me. I couldn't bear anything but the rage that was bone-deep for a family that took everything from me.

The Sokovs.

I released the velvet drapes with a scrunched nose, disgusted by the comfort they tried to bring me. No, there'd be no more comfort under the dutiful gaze of Lev and Leo Solkov.

Leo had become detached from the character he played late last night. His once gentle touch and playful smile were now shadowed with rage and exhaustion. It was like the curtain had dropped, and my stranger had become himself again—his true identity. I wanted to tear my skin off and throw it into the hearth and watch it burn. The treacherous skin that his lips had touched and his fingers had caressed.

Lev had dragged me up the stairs and dropped me here upon Leo's request. They might have been brothers, but it was obvious that one of them was in charge, and it was *not* the junkie. After pushing me into the polished room of books, he snarled. "Can you even read?"

"Can you go a day without a blow?" I rebutted without turning around.

And that's how we'd left things.

I'd spent the following morning hours searching through stacks of leather-bound books in various languages, genres, and stages of decay. My heartbeat was loud and erratic, and I closed my eyes as the tears came over me. I'd been up here for quite a while, and my body was telling me what it wanted and craved. I decided to push it down and keep exploring.

I took a deep breath before moving on. Though the library was well-stocked, it needed a lot of love. Some of the older books in the back were oxidized from age, and I was afraid to touch them for fear of the pages turning to dust.

I pulled a crumbling copy of Jane Eyre from the stacks and gasped. It was a first edition written under her pen name, Currer Bell. My thumb passed over the raised spine, and I couldn't help but smile in delight at being able to hold such a treasure. However, my joy dimmed when I thought of the similarities between Jane and me. The difference was that she chose not to marry the master of Thornfield Hall while I was being dragged to the altar by the master of this very library.

I could play the obedient wife who nods her head and bends over when asked, but that would spit in the face of the family. I can't remember that lies in unmarked graves somewhere—the brother who feels nothing but hate and a drive to right the wrongs of our previous generation. No, I don't think I'll go quietly to the altar. *'If people were always kind and obedient to those who are cruel and unjust, the wicked people would have it all their way; they would never feel afraid, and so they would never alter but would grow worse and worse.'*

Oh, Emily - what a woman you painted. What a woman I wished I could be.

Right then, I decided to use the library to distract myself and focus on something other than my rotting life. Maybe if I could save these books, I'd feel better about being unable to protect myself. I cleaned and restored one novel at a time until this entire room was an altar to the life I wanted for myself.

I placed the book carefully back on the shelf and moved on to the next aisle of novels when a soft melody caught my attention. It was slow, coming from down the hall I'd been told *not* to explore.

I looked over my shoulder towards the staircase, knowing either brother could march up and throw me into a room anytime. But the shaking in my hands drove me down the hall like an animal searching for water. Leo hadn't said much to me before he left, but he made sure I saw the locked liqueur cabinet and told me he was the only one who could open it.

Fucking bastard.

No, I didn't need to ask Leo for alcohol - or anything for that matter. I took a shaky before inching my way towards the melody. Most of the doors on this level were open, revealing a multitude of guest rooms in various styles and sizes,s but the melodic sound of a piano was from behind a barely cracked door. I inched around the door frame and looked into the dimly lit room, seeing the shirtless back of a man at the piano.

His tan skin was littered with scars, primarily small slashes with no pattern, but others were small holes - burn marks. Part of me wanted to feel bad for the man, but I knew better than that. I knew what men like him did to people - to families.

His shoulders tensed as his arms pulled in to play what sounded like Stravinsky, a famous Russian ballet composer. A smile washed across my face as the muscles in my legs flexed - memories of an open dance studio and not another soul in sight.

When I inched closer, though, the floor below me creaked, and the music suddenly stopped. The man's head lifted, his hands resting on the ivories before he grunted, "I know it's you, *milyy*."

"Lev," I said quizzically as I pushed the door open to see him frowning.

"What is it? Decided to admit you can, in fact, *not* read?" He teased me before grabbing a half-smoked cigarette from the seat beside him and lighting it. "Or are you just determined to make my life difficult?"

I crossed my arms and leaned against the door frame. "I heard the music playing and came to see who it was."

"Surprise," he muttered before inhaling the smoke.

I furrowed my brow before looking around the rest of the room. It starkly contrasted the other magazine-ready suites down the hall. The walls were painted a light gray, with various art pieces hung in different styles. Many of the works were abstract - all of the women with hard lines and sad expressions.

"Did you need something?" He asked me, exasperated, and my mouth opened before closing. "Leo won't be back for a few hours, but if you're bored . . ." He trailed off suggestively, and my nose wrinkled.

"Not even in your dreams."

He shook his head as a plume of smoke escaped his lips. "Oh *milyy*, it would certainly be my nightmares."

I stood up straight, trying not to stare at the continuing scars that littered his chest and arms. "Stravinsky isn't easy," I stated - almost in appreciation.

Lev's head tilted before he nodded. "Right. Ballet girl."

I looked down at the floor, suddenly feeling self-conscious. We both continued to stay silent, myself shuffling from one leg to the other before he motioned for me to either speak or get out. I hadn't thought about asking Lev for alcohol, but if anyone were going to give it to me, it would be him.

I cleared my throat before looking over my shoulder again, ensuring Leo wouldn't appear on the floor like a Gothic monster. "I'm not feeling well."

I looked back towards him, and his brow was raised, teeth clamped around the burning cigarette. "Oh?"

I nodded, my hands clenching at my sides as I tried to swallow my pride. "Do you have anything?"

Lev's lips curled wickedly as he put out the light. The muscles in his upper back strained as he turned to face me. "I need you to say what you want. Clearly."

I huffed.

"Fine, then. I'm afraid I can't help you."

"Wait." I uncrossed my arms and took a breath. "I need a drink - just something to hold me over until I can ween myself off."

He stared at me, dark eyes roaming my face like he was searching for something. We looked each other up and down, neither of us wanting to be the next one to break the silence. Finally, after several minutes, his head dropped, and he roughly scratched the back of his head.

"You know, Leo could help you -."

"Like he's helped you?"

He tightened his jaw but laughed. "Yeah. Okay."

I sighed. "I'm sorry, okay? I'm just trying not to crawl out of my skin here, and I don't want to talk with Leo about this. Or about anything really."

Lev nodded. "Yeah, I get that."

We stood in silence again, but it didn't last long. He stood from his piano bench and gently lifted the lid, putting out a small bottle of vodka and handing it over to me with equally shaky fingers.

"Don't tell him about this, yeah? He wouldn't understand."

I promised I wouldn't and turned to leave the room, but he stopped me.

"Ana?"

I turned.

"You have to know he isn't doing this to hurt you. He doesn't want any more of your family's blood on his hands."

I poked my tongue into my cheek and stayed silent. Leo and Lev's father had taken everything from me, and the worst thing was that I couldn't even remember what I'd been robbed of.

"He wanted Alexei to see reason, but tension got high in Chicago and with the bleeding crosses . . ." Lev trailed off, his eyes cast somewhere over my shoulder.

I sighed. "Leo knew what he was doing when he invited me into bed.

I might not remember my family being mascaraed, but that? I can't trust him. I can't trust anyone."

"Yeah," He winced. "That wasn't a part of the plan."

I huffed. "What *was* the plan? Lure me into the dark park and kidnap me?"

He smiled. "Something like that."

I rolled my eyes and turned back to leave, but again, Lev stopped me. "*Milyy*, this doesn't need to be difficult."

My hand was braced on the door frame, and I gripped it tighter. "Things became difficult the moment I arrived at the orphanage, Lev. Everything after that has just been life."

I left the room before he could stop me again and closed the door behind me, my hand gripping the bottle of spirits to my chest as I tried to breathe. Lev attempted to appear kind, but I knew it was to keep me docile. Keep me compliant and easier to manage. Still, he did give me the alcohol, and I knew he wouldn't want Leo to know about it.

Whether he knew it or not, it was leverage.

I quickly returned to the library and closed the heavy doors, leaning against them when the silence made me feel safe. Living on the streets of New York, I rarely heard the sound of silence. There was always a screaming voice, car horns blaring from streets away, or music from restaurants clawing their way into my brain, making breathing impossible. But when the alcohol hit my tongue, it was as close as I could get to peace.

I unscrewed the cap to the nip bottle and brought it to my lips, a sense of calm overtaking me the second I swallowed the contents of the plastic container in one swallow. The familiar burn coated my throat, my shaking hands setting the empty bottle beside me as I closed my eyes.

God, what had I done to myself? That I rely on that *poison* to live? When had it stopped being a fun distraction and turned into a tonic for my fried nerves?

Somewhere between cold nights on the streets and nightmares of a red-haired lady who I now know as Mom, I created a monster inside of me that fed on destruction.

Self-destruction.

After a few minutes, I felt my fingers still, my heartbeat dissipated, and the heavy fog in my mind started to clear. I felt human again.

My eyes opened and roamed over the beautiful room in front of me that was quiet, clean, and safe.

Though I knew that I'd always be my self-destruction, I only ever felt safe with myself.

I was predictable.

Other humans were not, and the Sokov brothers were hazardously human.

Ana

I hadn't realized I'd fallen asleep until I felt the book in my hands being removed. My eyes fluttered open to see the dark eyes of Leo, his face still a wash of mystery and curiosity. He was standing over me in a solid black, three-piece suit with a green tie that matched the couches in the library.

I had to close my mouth to keep the drool from seeping out.

Fuck, he always looked good.

He looked over the leather-bound edition of Anna Karenina in its original Russian writing and smiled.

"I didn't know how fluent you'd be."

I straightened in the plush chair and swallowed. "The nuns were thorough."

That was an understatement.

The clergy and nuns of St. Basil's were ruthless in our schooling, and I was appreciative of it. Instead of being a poor, ill-read orphan with no prospects, I was gifted with knowledge of exactly how fucked my situation was and a library full of classic literature while in the home.

"You said that last night while trying to hide the fact that you grew up in an orphanage. You had the same response; My *schooling was thorough.*"

Leo chuckled to himself. "My father couldn't have cared less about how well-read I was or if I even enjoyed learning anything other than the business of New York. If he saw me here with a book in my hand, he'd replace it with a knife and tell me to get my hands dirty. Like a man."

I swallowed. "Family game night must have been a blast."

His eyes sparkled, and he nodded. "They were . . . Intense."

"Poor baby *bratva*," I said with as much venom as I could muster.

He frowned. "It was rougher for Lev, being the youngest. He was always compared to me, which wasn't fair. He was expected to be as ruthless, skilled, and relentless as myself without a crown to call his own. He was always second best - and I wouldn't wish that upon any set of brothers."

He quickly pushed the emotions from his face as if he didn't mean to say all of that. Leo was anything if not detached. He only seemed to let himself out in the bedroom, and I winced at the idea of having to share a bed with him again.

Growing up in an orphanage was a lot like having siblings but without any of the love. We were all competing against one another for the attention of our matron, the best bed in the room, or even a new set of clothing. For those involved in ballet, it was even worse. How well you performed on stage equated to the care Matron Yulia would give you for the next month.

Leo set the book beside him as he sat across from me. The room was dark now, and I couldn't see the oak grandfather clock from here as my vision had disintegrated since leaving the home. "Do you have the time?"

Leo looked over his shoulder at the very same clock and squinted. "Half past nine."

I'd been hidden in this room all day.

"Have you not been shown to a guest room, or do you just prefer the loveseat?" A smirk tugged at his lips, and I rolled my eyes.

I smoothed my hands over the dark green fabric of the antique furniture and let myself smile. "Lev pointed toward a few rooms I could choose from, but I could honestly fall asleep anywhere these days. A subway seat, park bench, diner . . ."

I hadn't meant it to sound so depressing, but the crease between Leo's brows made me clear my throat. "The time just got away from me," I added.

He nodded. "It seems we have that in common."

I quirked my brow at him, but he didn't elaborate. I imagine a *bratva vor* had little time to himself, especially in a city that didn't sleep. If he's as important as I think, then his life doesn't belong to himself. It belonged to the brotherhood.

"The wedding will be in three days."

My head snapped up. "Excuse me?"

Leo reached into the pocket of his suit and pulled out a small, blue ring box, the latch made out of bronze. It looked like it came from a Victorian movie set, and when he tried to hand it to me, I couldn't move.

He sighed, setting it on the couch cushion before leaning back and crossing his legs indifferently. "If you don't like it, we can find something else."

"I haven't seen it yet, so how can I know if I don't like it?" My voice was robotic and stiff. The peace I had found in the library washed away like a broken dam.

I reached over and gently touched the box, my fingers running over it like the contents would jump out and bite me.

Three days.

It rang in my head like a death sentence.

"The tailor will be here tomorrow morning to fit you in a few gowns of your choosing, and you'll need to pick one from her existing line as we don't have time to make you one. She will also have a cataloger of clothes for you to pick from, and using your measurements, she'll ship the wardrobe here for you. "

Everything seemed so far away - muted and diluted by the sensation of being underwater.

Drowning.

"Ana?"

I looked up, my expression blank as he angrily stood from his chair and turned about the room. "You're not listening to me."

I snapped. "Does it matter?"

He turned and waved his hands towards the door. "I think it's time for you to retire for the night."

I laughed, clutching the ring box so hard it hurt. "The first day of the rest of my life." I was pushed into a solitary room and out of view.

Leo sighed, his cold demeanor crumbling. "There was never going to be another life for you, Ana. Not really. As the daughter of Nicholas Romanov, you never would have had a say in your life."

"I guess we'll never know, will we? Your father took that away from me long ago." My cold gaze sliced through him, and he took a step back.

His expression was cold - detached. "Do you think this is how I wanted my life to be?"

I snorted, turning away from him before I heard his footsteps across the hardwood. His hand shot out and wrapped around my chin, yanking my head up so I could stare into his black eyes.

Endless darkness.

"We were born into this destiny, and there's never been another way out. You can either clench your teeth and take it or bend beneath the pressure and let it bury you alive." His hands were rough, uncaring, and cold as he growled down at me. *No man or woman born, coward or brave, can shun his destiny.*

"Bend or break," I muttered, but Leo shook his head.

"I don't want you to bend to me, Ana. I want you to kneel." His eyes gleamed with desire, and I sneered.

"Circe crawls into bed with a handsome stranger, except he isn't a stranger!" I barred my teeth at him, fingernails curling into my palm. "You knew who I was when you put me on my knees, and for that, I'll never forgive you. I can't trust you."

Leo was silent, his beautiful face a picture of still perfection while I raged like a storm. When he opened his mouth, it sounded like the devil himself had come through him - taunting me.

"What does it say about you, Ana, that you were more willing to open up to a stranger than a man offering you a home, protection, and the life you were always destined to have? Do you think you would have had a choice with dear old Nikki as your father? No - he would have sold you to the highest bidder just as he was prepared to do with Olga before -".

I squinted at him. "*Olga*? Was she . . . Was she my sister?"

He grunted, swallowing harshly before responding. "The oldest."

"You know, I think it's time I retire for the night," I said in barely a whisper, fighting the tears that broke against my eyes like waves against a ship.

We stood very still, his fingers pressing my skin before he leaned in. I could smell his amber cologne and the streets of New York that clung to him like damp snow.

"*So, surrender to sleep at last. What a misery, keeping watch through the night, wide awake — you'll soon come up from under all your troubles.*"

I frowned. "*There is a time for making speeches and going to bed.*"

His eyes searched my own, dark brows pulled together in contemplation. "You're too intelligent to be the woman you want everyone to believe you are."

"And you're too heartless to see the damage you've inflicted on others."

I drew back from him and was grateful that he took a few steps back from me. Towering in the center of the dark library, he looked like a green statue, ordained in mortal clothes that only helped hide his true form. He had organic opulence that clung to his bones and came out of his pores.

I hated him.

I hated the man he pretended to be and the one he forced me to interact with. Was there a version of Leo that I could learn to live with?

Without another word, he turned on his heels and left the room, leaving the library doors wide open and me with an even more profound chasm of confusion about Leo Solkov.

I stood up once his footsteps dissipated back down the hall, picking up the novel I'd been reading earlier and setting the ring box atop it before exiting my favorite room of the house, but now I no longer feel isolated and safe. Leo had a way of leaching those feelings from a place.

Ana

I wandered down the hall, my head poking into the dark rooms that I was meant to make my own. The wall sconces in the hall were dimly lit, casting shadows onto the oil paintings and portraits that lined both sides. Each one looked old, ornate, and posh to the point of sickening. I wanted to take a can of red paint across each upturned face to remind them of the blood it took to build their legacy. Their fortune.

My chest cracked at the realization that my family had apparently been no better. As a *vor*, my father would have had to do horrendous things to keep his throne. Horrendous things that would lead to him being overthrown and the death of his wife and children.

All but two.

I didn't even know all of their names. *"Olga,"* I tested how the word rolled off my tongue and tugged at my heart's broken and rigid pieces.

Leo said she was the eldest of us, with Alexei being the last of the Romanovs to enter this world. I wondered if he remembered more than I did or was just as clueless and lost. The images from Chicago did not paint the picture of a scared or broken little boy, though.

No.

They told the Solkovs that a day of reckoning was upon us, and New York would see his face again. I held onto that idea, not thinking of the army of *bratva* men who'd sworn their lives to Leo. If I were ever going to see my brother, it would be by the grace of Vor Leonid Solkov.

I stepped up to a dark room across from Lev's; my hands braced on the wall beside the door as my teeth dug into my lip. It would only be a matter of time before my hands started shaking again, and the sound of my own heart overtook the thoughts in my head. But how long would Lev let this go on?

I peered into the dark room, music echoing softly on a record player. How pathetic was I that I needed to tiptoe around Lev, a man I loathed, in hopes that he'd slip me alcohol?

Terribly pathetic.

But desperate.

I moved to go into the dark guest room when the door to his room slowly opened, revealing a now fully clothes Lev with a bored expression on his handsome face. Unlike Leo, Lev was a man who wore his trauma on his sleeves, the red tinge to his eyes and hollow cheeks admitting more than he ever could.

"Lurking, *printsessa*?"

I didn't even try to sugarcoat it as my tongue wet my lips, and his eyes watched me. "If I don't have anything before bed -."

He interrupted. "You'll wake up in a cold sweat?"

I nodded.

Lev opened his bedroom door a little wider, and I swallowed. "Leo is home."

His brow quirked. "Is he? It's rather early for him," he said while checking his wristwatch.

"He found me in the library." I held up the book with the ring box atop it, and he nodded in understanding.

"You open it yet?"

I shook my head, staring down at the ground in hopes of hiding the look of despair that likely lined my face. I don't know if I could open it - Leo would probably have to slide it on my finger during the ceremony, and even then, I doubt I could look at it for too long.

A wedding ring.

It was a death sentence to my sanity but a chance of life for a brother I didn't know. Even if it saved Alexei's life, I would no longer be his lost little sister. I would be the wife of the man sitting on *his* family throne. There would be no future for my brother and I. We were at the mercy of Leo Solkov, just as our father was at the mercy of Vlad Solkov.

Lev opened his door wider and sighed when he saw my hesitation. "He'll be in his office until midnight - if not longer."

I stood when I asked, "Why are you helping me?"

He chuckled, leaning against the door frame so his arms tugged at the white button-up that clung to his body. "Us addicts gotta stick together."

I scoffed, taking a step back and taking a step back towards the library when he reached out and grabbed my upper arm - much gentler than how Leo did.

"Wait."

I looked down at where his fingers touched me, and he let go. "I guess I know how it feels to not be in control."

I turned around to face the man, his body rigid as the admissions made him feel exposed. But that's how both brothers made me feel - laid bare and at their mercy.

"I didn't ask for any of this."

He nodded. "Yeah, none of us ever do."

Sighing, I dropped my arms and nodded towards his open door. He stepped back into the room and gave me a tight smile as I walked in, leaving it cracked behind us. A dim lamp was sitting beside his bed, illuminating the many pieces of art on his walls, and my eyes settled on one streaked with dark blue, his chin jutting upwards as if held, and eyes left a vacant white - staring down at me.

Lev was going through a small box beside the piano when he lifted a pipe, grinder, and lighter. I shook my head, "I was really just looking for something to -."

"Yeah, but you can't keep that up. After the wedding, you'll be expected to attend meetings and sit with the other wives, and when you get pregnant, it'll all have to stop."

I stepped back as if slapped. "Excuse me?"

Lev's face dropped. "Well, you can't drink with a baby, Ana, and going cold turkey could be even more dangerous."

"Who said there's to be a baby? Leo never said anything to me about getting pregnant." My heart raced as my fight or flight senses told me to leave - run for the door no matter the cost. Something cold inside of me curled around my heart and gripped it tight - a memory playing in my mind that I wasn't ready to relive.

Lev grimaced before sighing. "Forget I said anything, but alcohol still isn't something you can hide very well. You can start cutting the cravings with weed for now, and it's not addictive, so when you - when you want to stop, you can."

I'd smoked before, but it never had the same effect alcohol had. While weed tended to make me overthink, liqueur took the evil thoughts away. Yeah, I could see how weed was better in the long run, but the church was much more strict on drugs, legal or not, while alcohol was shared openly.

"You can't hide it from Leo for much longer."

I winced. "I suspect he already knows."

"He always does." He outstretched his hand, the pipe and lighter sitting there, and my fingers started to twitch.

"It takes the edge off?"

"For a while at least," he admitted.

I reached over and took the glass pipe that was already packed and held it tight before bringing it to my lips. Before lighting it, I stopped. "You still have alcohol, though, right?"

Lev gave me a knowing look, his eyes squinting before he nodded in understanding.

The moment I inhaled, I felt my body relax. It didn't fill me with the same warmth that drinking did, but it was better than going through life without anything. I cough once, taking a breath of fresh air before passing the pipe back to a curious Lev.

"Feel a little better?"

I smiled. "Yeah, and the vodka?"

My body felt calm, but there was still something it craved more than the silence that substances gave me. I need that familiar burn, the heat pooling in my belly like arousal and the serenity that washed over me when I drank.

Lev replaced the pipe with a shot glass of vodka, and I scoffed. "A Russian running low on vodka?"

He wasn't amused, simply clinking his shot glass to mine before we both swallowed our prescribed dose of poison for the night. The vodka fought the sensation of being high, both dimming my nerves and making the world a lot less loud.

More inhabitable for a person like me - plagued with half-memories and vivid nightmares.

Setting the glass atop the piano, I couldn't keep the smile off of my face as weed made me feel untroubled - in a different way than alcohol did. My fingers skimmed across the ivories, pressing on a high note and humming in enjoyment.

"Do you play?"

I peeked up at Lev through hooded eyes and shook my head. "No, but I'd become intimately connected to the piano through my years of ballet." My lips pursed as the Le Réveil de Flore melody played in my head. "I miss the stage, oddly enough."

"I've never played for another besides Leo and my mother - the thought of eyes watching me as I pour my soul out through an instrument makes me feel ill." He shook his head as the idea burned just as much as the alcohol in our systems.

I nodded in agreement but then quickly shook my head. "It's different for me," I sniffed before smiling. "The orphanage always felt like a grand opera house where I tried to impress people - please people. The stage was the only place that felt real. When the lights are on, you can't even see the crowd. It's just you, the music and the pain."

"Pain?"

I looked up at Lev's confused face. "Oh yes, there was a lot of pain. Sometimes, it was all you could think about. The dance is ingrained into your memory through sensations - nerve endings set on fire when you know you're doing something right. When it got bad enough that my legs screamed, my arms shook, and my back ached - the rest of the world faded away. I guess I replaced that pain with alcohol."

He ran a hand through his hair, much shorter than his brother's, eyes the color of whiskey, whereas Leo's were obsidian. "The piano was the only place there *wasn't* a pain in my life," he admitted.

I thought about what Leo said - Lev being the youngest and constantly having to prove himself just to end up second best. I can see how it'd drive someone to drugs just to numb it all - or give him enough energy to keep fighting through his hellish family dynamic.

"My father hated that I would rather pick up a paintbrush than a gun. It all came so naturally to Leo." A slight bitterness was behind his voice, and I felt for him. He was an asshole, but we were all products of our environment.

Even Leo.

"The paintings are sad," I mainly commented to myself as my eyes roamed the room. My mouth seemed to be a whole lot looser under weed than alcohol, surprisingly. "But they feel real."

I looked at Lev, a pair of painted eyes peering down at me from just above his head. "Isn't it funny how sadness is the most shared emotion we can feel?"

Lev watched me briefly, his eyes boring holes into the back of my head before he cleared his throat. "You should probably get to bed."

I nodded my head absently. "Don't be afraid to feel sad, Lev."

Turning around, I looked at his confused face and smiled sadly. "It takes courage to feel sad when the world tells you to be happy."

Leaving him with that, I left his room and fell onto the guestroom floor in a tired heap, thinking of a time I allowed myself to feel anything at all.

Ana

I was roused from my stupor just as the sun kissed the horizon, melting away the frost that had settled on the double pain windows of the Solkov townhome. Half asleep, Lev had barged into the guest suite to announce that the tailor would be there any minute. He didn't wait for a reply as he slammed the door, making my teeth rattle.

"That frame! *Très français*, Ana." Ambre clasped her hands around my shoulders as her assistant measured me.

I forced myself to smile, not wanting to admit that my French figure was due to living on the streets and not having a reliable food source.

The small French woman pursed her lips as my shoulders slumped. We had tried on four dresses, and my reaction to them had all been the same. "This one is fine."

She shook her head and muttered, *"Ces épouses russes."*

The truth was that all the dresses *had* been fine, but each one was just another reminder that I was days away from marching down the aisle and into a life of chains and heartbreak. There would be no happy ending for me - I wasn't the Disney princess getting a happily ever after with a mysterious prince.

I was being blackmailed into a union that could stop a war but also ensure that the brother I meant to save would never see me as a sister. I would be the traitor who married into the family that killed off the

Romanovs and now meant to keep us under their thumb.

"This one is okay?" I sighed into my hands, head hanging low as the reflection in the mirror sneered at me.

"O.K? *Non*, this is not o.k. This is silk! This is Valentine!"

She continued to argue with her assistant in French as I walked off the pedestal, still wearing the long satin dress that clung to my body like a second skin. The sleeves were to my wrist, the neckline high across my collar, and the train flowed behind me as I made my escape.

I held the light fabric between my fingers as I slipped around the corner, running right into a hard wall of Armani.

"Fucking hell!" I groaned as my ass hit the high polished wooden floor of the hallway.

"I have to admit, *Circe*, you really do look better when you're kneeling."

I could feel myself blush as my eyes landed on his olive-toned face, his hair well-done and pushed back as he reached down to help me from the floor.

I slapped his helped away and huffed. "It's bad luck to see the bride in her dress before the wedding day."

Leo smiled, looking over my shoulder to the bickering stylists who'd barely noticed my absence. "I think we have enough black clouds following us, Ana. What's one more?"

Standing on my wobbly legs, I braced myself against the hallway wall, looking up at the groom with annoyance. "I wasn't expecting to see you today."

He was fixing the cuffs of his jacket, not meeting my gaze. "I have to keep you on your toes." His gaze roamed over my silhouette as he smirked. "Or your knees."

My body shivered, and I hated myself for it. "So what do you want? To see if my suffering brings you as much joy as it does, Lev?" I sneered.

The younger brother had peaked into the room a few times, his eyes alight with mischief as I was poked and squeezed into the last few dresses. *"Have the frogs tortured you enough for today, dear?"* Lev had said to be in Russian as the seamstress pinned a strap in place.

I smiled. *"I do well under torture, pig. You are best to remember that."*

He had laughed and slid out of the room.

Leo's shoulders tensed as he looked down the hall. "Is Lev bothering you often?"

I snorted. "I think it's a mutual *bothering*."

He nodded his head, looking back at me and grunting. "I won't be home tonight, and you likely won't see me until the wedding."

I raised a brow. "And how did I get so lucky?"

"I have a business that requires my attention and can't do it in the city. Lev and a few other staff members will be here while I'm gone."

"Our staff?"

He sighed. "Yes, Ana. You'll be the lady of the house and should get used to running it. Yulia will be preparing meals - she says you're more than welcome to keep her company if my brother becomes too much."

Lady of the *house*? What fucking century did he think we were in that I would waltz around his home with a clattering of keys, following me into every room like a Tudor Queen?

"I'm more than happy in the library."

"I know you are, but meeting the people who work for you might be good."

I winced.

I didn't want to meet these people who were jail wardens. They were here to keep an eye on me, keep me occupied, or keep me captive. None of them were actually interested in getting to know me.

Well, maybe Lev was. But that was only because he had finally found someone with a more fucked up life than himself.

"I'll keep that in mind," I bit out.

Leo sighed, checking his watch before looking back at me with something akin to regret. "I wouldn't be leaving if it wasn't necessary."

I cocked my head and laughed. "You think I *care* if you'll be here or not? I might sleep better knowing my captor isn't under the same roof."

His nostrils flared as he tried to calm himself. I could see the walls of his perfectly built demeanor start to crumble. "You agreed to this - for Alexei. Don't give me a reason to regret this arrangement that is becoming far more trouble than it's worth."

I grinned. "And watch the streets of New York run red with Solkov blood? That doesn't sound too bad."

I flinched as Leo stepped forward, his arm reaching out, grasping my thin neck in his hand just hard enough to keep me in place. I could smell his shampoo, soft and light, fighting with his natural musk that was sharp and heavy. "*Lisichka,* where is the little obedient woman I had just nights ago? We'd had so much fun together."

I straightened my chin, my body shaking as his chest pressed against mine. "Where's the man who promised me pleasure? Since waking up in your arms, I've felt nothing but darkness. Who really changed here?"

Leo's thumb brushed my lower lip, the smell of his toothpaste surrounding me as I fought myself over what I would do if he leaned down and kissed me. I liked to think I could pull away - slap him and march back into the room, but I wasn't daft. I knew that when it came to this man. This insufferable and horrid man, that my body betrayed me.

"*We men are wretched things.*"

I hissed, "Indeed."

"I can see the fight behind your eyes, *Circe.* I can see your witchling wanting to escape and play with me. Why won't you let her?"

I sucked in a breath, and when I did, he pushed his thumb into my mouth and pressed down on my treacherous tongue. I involuntarily moaned around his finger, my eyes fluttering as his knee moved between my thighs.

"We can come to an arrangement, Ana. One that could benefit us both."

My eyes opened, staring up at his obsidian gaze that tore through me with precision. He pulled his thumb back, my tongue darting out to flick across it before he wiped it over my bottom lip.

I swallowed. "I thought we already had an arrangement?" One that I was wrestling with myself for making in the first place.

He smiled, eyes alight as he peered down at me. "A different sort of arrangement. One that only brings us . . ." He paused for a moment to search for the word. "Rapture."

My face was still trapped in his grasp, my eyes forced to look up into his, and my body encased in his warmth. "I'm listening."

Leo leaned forward so that his cheek was against mine and his lips were to my ear. His hand lowered again to rest against my neck. "I could see how eager you were to let go with me, Ana. I could feel the need inside of you to be anyone but the woman who carries the weight of a family on your shoulders." His fingers brushed under my chin, moving my head to the side as his lips met my neck.

"You can fight me as you please as Ana, but *Circe* will kneel in the bedroom. You'll call me, sir, when there's no one around to hear your moans. This fight that you have to hate me while also wanting me can end - and you can have both. Would you like that, *Lisichka?*"

Shivers ran down my body, though I felt his warmth encasing me. I had felt so relieved to give up my power - hand it over to the stranger who promised me pleasure and safety. The stranger could be trusted, but my future husband could not.

"Can it really be that simple?"

He hummed, "There's nothing simple about us, Ana, but this could be. I could make it easy. Even if it's only when the sun goes down, I want you to be mine. I want you to submit to me, but I understand the fight inside of you and how it clashes with the need to let go. Let go,

Ana."

I nodded, tears escaping me as my tired soul gave way to Leo. "Yes."

He growled, "Yes, what?"

"Yes, sir. Yes, my *stranger*."

His lips were on me in an instant, pouring his frustration into every nip of his teeth and lash of his tongue as I crumbled in his arms. Nothing about my life had ever been simple or easy, but this could be. It had to be because I feared that this man could be the ruin of me. He could be my savior or my damnation. My captor and my fallen angel. I just had to let go. Let. Go.

His hands found my breast through the soft silk, teasing my nipple with gentle strokes as I moaned into his mouth and trembled beneath his touch. His other hand was supporting my lower back as my legs threatened to give out below me, and his knee pushed between my thighs and radiated a delicious warmth that settled on my core.

All too soon, Leo pulled away from me and audibly moaned at the loss of his warmth against me, my eyes still shut while his hands around my back kept me secure but at a safe distance away from him.

"I have to go, but I'll see you in the church."

My eyes opened to see that the dark stranger was gone, and the Solkov *vor* was back again. His face was a mask of stone, unyielding as always.

I sniffed, straightening up and smoothing my hands over the wrinkled silk. "Like I said, it'll help me rest knowing you're not lurking around every corner."

A shadow of a smirk crossed his lips before he stepped away from me and let his eyes roam my body.

"That one."

I looked down at the cream-colored fabric and sighed. "It's Valentine, so I'm told."

"It's perfect."

Without another word, he turned and left me standing in the hall, my face a mess of silently shed tears and my lips bruised - more so than my ego.

A creaking floorboard had my head turning down the dark hall just in time to see Lev's door click close.

* * *

Ambre had left after many more hours of her inditing that I needed to choose more than a couple outfits from her catalogs, feeling only relieved when I told her that *'Mr. Solkov has requested the Valentine'.*

I was now hidden away in the library, my fingers trembling below a yellowed page of Pride and Prejudice from the 19th century and likely belonged behind a glass pain. I sighed, throwing my head back against the chair and forcing my lungs to take a deep, measured breath. It was now midday, and I hadn't had an ounce of alcohol - and my body was reminding me of why I never did that.

I didn't want to slink to Lev's door again and ask pathetically for my daily dose of poison after he witnessed my pathetic display with Leo this morning. For some reason, it is wrong for Lev to have seen us in that way—a betrayal of the uneasy truce that the youngest brother and I had built together.

Like summoning the devil himself, the library door opened, and Lev stepped through. He wore his signature black slacks, a loose-fitting button-up that he had rolled to the elbows, and a loose smile on his lips.

"So we have the house to ourselves for a few days."

I closed my book and set it beside me on the couch, raising a brow at his uncharacteristically easy attitude. It usually took finding him behind a piano with drugs in his system for him to appear so calm.

"Leo says that other staff members will start showing their faces around the house, so naturally, I'll be secluding myself from the library until you have to drag me down the aisle."

He laughed, closing the oak doors behind him as he lazily walked into the light that shined in from the open French windows. When the beams of yellow rays hit his eyes, they looked like honey, surrounded by drug-agitated red veins.

"So you spoke with Leo before he left?" He asked as his fingers swept over the nearest bookshelf, his eyes not meeting mine.

I crossed my arms over my chest and cocked my head. "Yes, but you already know that."

"What else did he say?" He continued to pace around the room like a lost animal, looking up at the ceiling and not knowing what to do with his hands.

"He wanted to talk about some expectations after the wedding."

"Hm," he hummed before finally stopping before me with his hands in his pockets.

What was the matter with him? Even if he had seen the entire confrontation with Leo, it didn't make sense why he acted so dodgy about it. He was the one who caught me trying to escape this house after having a wild night with the *vor*. I sighed, putting my shaking hand to my cheek as my body trembled.

God, I really needed something.

This seemed to catch Lev's attention, and his brows raised to look at me. "Need a hit?"

I shook my head. "Weed makes me tired, and I don't need to ruin my sleep schedule on top of my crippling mental health. Maybe three days of cold turkey before the wedding will do me some good. Get it out of my system."

He laughed under his breath, "Like three days could do that."

"Then what else do you suggest?" I snapped at him.

Lev looked like he was going to say something but stopped as he stepped forward and awkwardly sat on the couch beside me. His hands rested firmly on his knees, and this close, I could see the agitation under his nose from his latest line.

"I've tried cutting it all out, and it nearly killed me. I know what you're thinking - how could it get much worse?" He looked over at me, and I frowned.

He chuckled. "I had to think of why I started using and if the situation had changed. Because if I was still in the same shitty life that drove me to drugs in the first place, then what was going to stop me from doing it again?"

I nodded, wrapping my gray sweater around me that Ambre had brought with her from samples. I was leaning back against the couch with my legs pulled in, looking at the youngest brother, who was trying to open up to me and wondering what I could say to ease his pain.

Especially when I couldn't ease my own.

"But if anything, things had gotten worse. When my father died, I thought I'd be free from the heavy cloud that had always followed me. Leo was my older brother and would surely understand that I wasn't cut out for this life, wouldn't he? I was in for a rude awakening when Leo Solkov took over the throne of New York - a younger and more bloodthirsty vor than his predecessors."

Lev sat back with his shoulders resting against the dark green couch, his eyes staring straight ahead.

"I think Leo had always hated how easy this life came to him. He loathed our father and the things he did to take and keep power but then turned around and did it tenfold when it was his turn. To be the person he always hated, he had to bury himself really, really far down." Lev turned to look at me now, and I could see the strain in his eyes. "And I could see the same thing happening to you if you let him."

I winced, my head turning away at his truth. Leo was already making me question who I was, what I wanted, and the lengths I was willing to go to keep myself afloat.

"Leo is trying to make this shitty situation work," I said, even though it tasted bitter on my tongue. "He and I have come to an agreement that could - lessen the tension."

Lev chuckled darkly. "Using you as a fuck toy. That's what you mean."

My face grew heated as I sat up straighter. "I would be using him just as much as he's using me."

"But he can handle it. He's already burned away everything that makes him human and replaced it with a creature meant to sit on his throne and cast judgment on those lesser than him. He's hardened himself, Ana. You're still - you still have a little hope inside of you."

I wiped away a stray tear that fell from my eyes and sighed. "So what am I supposed to do then? I don't think I'll be able to avoid Leo's bed, and when I can't, am I supposed to hate him still and make the experience miserable? You said it yourself, Lev, that none of us has a choice."

I felt his warm hand on my leg, a touch so light you could barely tell it was there. I looked up at the walls torn away from his face and the shadow of a boy who just wanted to paint and play piano all day while his father used him as a soldier. His dark hair was going in every direction, his eyes pleading and mouth set in a firm line that made me want to embrace him, but not out of romantic want. I needed a friend; I could tell it had been a long time since Lev had one.

"I don't have all of the answers, Ana. I love my brother and would die for my *vor*, but I can't keep quiet as I watch him pull you into a darkness you could avoid."

I placed my hand gingerly over Lev's and ignored his slight flinch, but he didn't pull away. I rubbed away my tears with the back of my hand and offered a small smile. "The darkness was already there, Lev. Maybe I could wield it for something useful instead of allowing it to use and consume me. Something worthy of our pain."

Leo

I clenched my hand as I walked down the steps of 1266 Cobble Hill, my skin still feeling the phantom warmth of her breast from below her silk wedding dress. Anastasia Romanov was a beacon of fire atop the library of Alexandria - a flashing warning that said, *Stay back, for I am dangerous yet alluring.*

When I'd seen her photo land on my desk last year, I thought I was staring at a ghost. Her sky-like eyes and auburn hair sang to me like a siren in the deep. I wanted to know how she felt, how she smelt, and if her cries were as sweet as I'd imagined.

They were.

I cursed under my breath at having to leave her before the wedding, my body aching to feel her against me again and hear her cries of ecstasy - yet I knew I was doing this for us. For the family, I was trying to create the power I needed to keep her safe.

I straightened my jacket as my driver eyed me from beside the car, his gaze switching to the blacked-out SUV with government plates across from my house.

I growled, "John fucking Davis."

When I stepped up to the car and saw his boyish grin, I wanted to reach through and pull him out by his throat.

"It's been a while, Mr. Solkov, and you haven't returned my calls."

Fuck.

I waved my hand off to Boris, who was eyeing the car from here, likely with a hand on his gun.

Getting into the governor's car, the security in the front sneered at me.

"Weapons," he demanded, to which I rolled my eyes and looked to Davis.

"I'm the one who got you elected. Do you think I'd go through all that trouble to assassinate you?"

Governor Davis waved off his security before we pulled into traffic.

"I don't need to ask if you've seen the news," Davis said, looking out the other window. He might be a man with a lot of power, but it wasn't natural. It was handed to him by the seven families, and he always did well to try to tiptoe around making any demands. I had a long list of whores and bastard children in my vault to make his name worthless, and he knew that.

"I have men in Chicago as we speak, but the reports are true. Alexei is working with the Italians."

"Fuck," Davis muttered.

I watched him dab sweat off his beat-red face, my hands digging into my pants as my patience wore thin.

"The reports coming out of Little Italy are worrying, Mr. Solkov. I have agents saying there's been an uptick in undocumented ships coming into New York from New Orleans with your red tape over everything. What exactly are you bringing into the city?"

I turned to him, my expression dark. "I'm doing what's necessary for my city, John. If you want to keep your little slice of Hallmark perfection, you'll stop looking into things that don't concern you."

The silver-spooned fuck could ruin everything I'd been working on.

"I don't like this. I will keep as many up-town as possible, but if guineas start rolling through 5th Ave with machine guns, then I will have to -".

My hand wrapped around the governor of New York's throat, the security in the front shouting and trying to reach behind his seat, but his fat ass couldn't unbuckle himself in time.

"It's been a stressful week, John, so maybe the details of our arrangement have become clouded. Let me clear some things up for you." My hand gripped the side of his neck - face turning red while the car started to pull over.

"You are a stand-in for the Bratva. *You* do nothing but take photos and open the Macy's Day parade. So when I tell you I have it handled, believe it's handled." I pushed off him and opened the car door, stepping out onto the streets while he tried to catch his breath.

I looked over my shoulder towards him and grinned, "Oh, and John? I'm getting married in two days, and the governor of New York needs to be there. For the cameras, you see? My people will be in touch."

I turned on my heel and started walking towards Cobble Hill, pulling out my phone to make a call. It rang twice before being picked up, "Sir?"

"Tell Mr. Lucchese I'll be late for our meeting. I have to make a detour."

Ana

I spent the rest of my day huddled in the library, too tired to deal with the new voices in the house or footsteps that would stomp through the bottom stories. Lev had told me that the staff was instructed to stay off of this floor, and I had a small sigh of relief when I could leave the room and tiptoe to Lev's room for a hit without getting caught.

The sun had already set, and the horizon glowed a deep pink before bowing to the dark nights that plagued New York during the winter. I had become accustomed to the long nights, cold wind, and head-splitting holiday music that could be heard across the Hudson, but I always missed the sun. Not the heat waves that would roll off the city pavement and melt you into the streets, but an early summer morning when the birds were loud, and the parks were filled with children laughing.

What a distant world that was.

I knocked quietly on the door that was usually left ajar and entered when I heard the piano stop. Lev was sitting at the bench with a marijuana cigarette between his lips and nodded when he saw it was me.

"Done hiding?"

I shook my head, cheekily plucked the cigarette from his lips, and brought it to my own, smiling at the crease between his brows. "I'd gotten used to strangers in my life, but it's different when they all know *me*. Soon to be mistress of the house," I said sarcastically before pulling the smoke into my lungs and holding it there.

"You're a lot more than the Solkov bride, Ana. You're a walking folklore to most of the community now."

I passed the burning stick back to him and raised a brow. "What do you mean?"

Lev rolled his eyes and took a drag himself, letting it out through his nose. "When the Romanovs were," he paused to look for the best word before settling on, "Dethroned. Everyone thought the children were gone, too. Yeah, there were rumors, but none of them really stuck until those bodies showed up in Chicago. Now that you're alive, you're an heir to one of the greatest bratva dynasties in the Americas. That and the empty seat -".

Lev froze momentarily, his eyes dashing to me before looking down at the ground.

"What seat?" I thought he couldn't possibly mean a seat at the *Bratskaya Semyorka,* but I was wrong.

"Historically, the seat has always passed to a male heir, but I doubt Alexei is willing to break bread with the men who helped take his throne. *If* Alexei is unwilling, and I'm sure he is, then the seat belongs to you - or rather your husband when you marry."

My hand snapped out and stopped himself from bringing the cigarette to his lips again. Lev's eyes watching me in shock as my voice was eerily calm. "This was never about Alexei then, was it? This was about Leo taking even more power in the *bratskaya semyorka.*"

The youngest brother of the Solkov *bratva* winced. "Neither of us wants that boy's blood on our hands. After the legacy our father left us with the rest of your family, it seemed like one more soul taken off our scales in the underworld if we could keep him alive."

"But," I said in barely a whisper.

He sighed. "But the seat would give Leo an advantage over the other *vors.*" He looked up at me, his whiskey eyes full of regret. "A near tyrannical advantage."

"I thought the Solkovs were already running Manhattan and Long Island. What more does he want?"

"The eastern seaboard," he admitted while rubbing his hand over the stubble on his chin. It cast a slight shadow over his already hollow features. "The seat of power in the east is here in New York, but the brotherhood rules from Montreal to Miami. No one has ever had more than one seat."

I'm sure Vors would rather marry off their daughters to nobodies than give more power to their enemies. The other brotherhood members might cooperate to ensure that Russians held the reigns, but what was the old saying? Keep your friends close, and your enemies . . .

"So he gets two out of the seven seats when we marry, and Alexei is still a pariah here in New York. His home."

Lev nodded grimly, turning fully on his piano bench and resting his elbows on his knees. He hung his head low, the steeples of the Orthodox church pointing directly at me like a threat.

"He runs the territory of New York - the most profitable territory in the Americas but not the most influential. The brotherhood has had to make some strict rules over the years to keep families from killing each other and becoming too powerful. You can only take more than one seat through marriage, not blood. When our father took New York, he gave up a vital part of the country and left it vacant for over a decade."

He looked up at me, his eyes squinting in what looked like pain as he rubbed his hands together, trying to bring life back into his body. "My father foolishly listened to a priest who told him New York was the seat of the church in the states and that it would bring him an almost holy power if he took it in the name of God." Lev laughed under his breath, "What a fucking fool."

"So your father relinquished a territory in exchange for New York, and it sat empty this long?"

He winced. "When we moved out, it left an opening for other families to move in. Families who didn't abide by the *bratskaya semyorka*."

"Then who?"

"Michael Lucchese, the don of Washington D.C."

My eyes widened. "Your father was the vor of a city filled with politicians and money and just abandoned it for a territory that already had a vor? Butchered a family for a seat that was already taken?"

He nodded. "All because a crazy priest told him about *Candy Mountain.*"

"So now Leo wants D.C., and I'm the one who can give it to him."

"You give Leo the rights to the territory, but we still have to win it back from the Luccheses, and they will not just hand it over with a fruit basket. You might be stopping a war in New York, but the ring on your finger will still be steeped in blood by the time this is all over."

I looked at my empty finger and thought of the ring box still untouched in the library. Such an innocent-looking box, but it was Pandora's, and I was about to release the evils of its contents onto the world.

"And what happens to the Lucchese family when Leo takes D.C.? Will there be tiny graves with no one to mourn them?" My voice was acidic, thinking of an old photo of four little girls adorned in their best dresses. "Will there be survivors to remember the horrors your brothers means to inflict on an innocent family?"

Lev was silent.

Of course not, because Leo had learned a lesson from his father.

No loose strings.

No Alexei Romanovs.

"If I marry Leo, I'm sentencing an entire family just as my own was. But if I don't marry Leo, then I'm signing a death certificate for my brother." I met Lev's eyes as a tear silently fell down my cheek. "What do I do?"

Lev stood up, towering over me and blocking out the light from his bedside lamp. I could see a soft glow around him, and his face was cast in shadows. He didn't say anything, just looking down at me with a mixture of regret and sympathy that I didn't want. I didn't need anyone's pity - I needed a solution.

Finally, he took a breath. "You have to convince Alexei to keep his seat."

I laughed under my breath. "Convince a man I don't know to make a truce with our family's murderers? Yeah, I'll get right on that."

"Think about it, Ana. When you marry Leo, it protects Alexei from the crosses but also clears a path for him to take his seat. If he takes it, he can stay in Chicago, and Leo can't move to D.C. The windy city has never had a *bratva*; the Italians and Irish have kept it for decades, but Alexei had managed to start from the ground. The brotherhood would welcome him with open arms if he brings Chicago to the table."

I sighed. "But what about D.C? Leo isn't going to let that go now that his mind is set on it. Even if I can convince Alexei to take the seat, what's to stop Leo from taking the city anyway."

"Like I said, there are rules. A vor can only take one city for one seat, and Leo will never give up New York. He can't move on D.C without starting a war with the *bratskaya semyorka*."

"Okay," I drawled out with a scoff. "But there's still the matter of Alexei. You don't behead six men if you're not set on starting a battle for New York. We still don't even know if he accepted the marriage. This would still blow up in Leo's face."

Lev hesitated momentarily, fighting an idea in his mind that struggled to break free. When it did, I wish he would have kept it to himself.

"You have to contact Alexei."

I flinched back from him, my hands twisting in front of me nervously.

I knew I'd eventually have to come face to face with my brother, but I never imagined it'd be to convince him to take his seat back.

"We don't know if he'll believe I'm his sister. He took six Solkov men, meaning he believes my life was taken, too. How are we supposed to make him see me?"

Lev reached out, catching a stray piece of my red hair and twisting it in. "He'll know."

Images of a laughing woman, a gold necklace, and bright blue eyes flashed in my mind. "I look like her."

He nodded. "I knew it the moment I saw you."

My eyes flickered up, and I tilted my head. "Did you know her? Did you know my family?"

He swallowed, shaking his head as if he meant to dislodge a memory. "I don't remember much - I was young when everything *happened*. But I'd seen her at parties, always with a child attached to her skirts and her red hair piled up in braids. That's all I know."

Liar.

He knew much more than he was willing to say, but why wouldn't he tell me? What more could he say about his family that could damage my outlook on the Solkovs? And if Lev wouldn't tell me, I knew Leo wouldn't.

My eyes squinted while his gaze tore away from me. He walked back to his piano bench, setting his hands gingerly on the keys before saying in a whisper. "He'll know."

And then he started to play, and he didn't stop playing until the sun rose above the brick houses of Cobble Hill.

Ana

"*S*ouriez, Ana! *S'il te plaît.* You can not go down the aisle looking so grim on your wedding day!" Ambre begged of me as she and two other assistants bound me in my wedding dress and piled my hair into a neat bun.

"I will smile when it's over," I muttered under my breath, but they all heard me, their eyes glancing between themselves in horror.

"So ungrateful," they whispered.

"Beauty is wasted on her. *Gaspillé,*" Ambre tutted from behind me as she fastened my hair in place.

I ignored them all, my hands shaking as I ran them over Leo's chosen dress. I now regretted letting him choose it, knowing that it was likely the only control I'd been allowed in this entire ordeal, and I had given it up to him so easily. I'd given him a lot of things easily.

My eyes stole a glance in the mirror, caked under layers of makeup to hide the dark circles that plagued me and the sallow look to my skin. My heartbeat was going about a million miles an hour, and I had to wonder if it was from a lack of alcohol or the fact that I was walking towards my doom any second.

A knock at the door tore my attention away from my thoughts.

"It's time, *milyy.*"

It certainly was.

When I stepped out of the brownstone for the first time in four days, the clouds above the city were a dark and ominous gray; it was the kind of sky that brought freezing rain, not whimsical snow. Lev looked up as he stepped beside me and cursed under his breath. "A storm wasn't on the radar for today."

I turned to him and gave a small smile. "Yes, it was."

Cobble Hill was lined with black SUVs, all ready for the parade to the church where I'd sign my life away in exchange for Alexei's. The barren trees reached towards the sky, dark branches twisting around power lines and coated in thin layers of ice. Though it was the twentieth of December, I could have sworn I was stepping into Sleepy Hollow, where headless horsemen would take me away any minute.

I might have preferred that.

The Holy Virgin Protection Orthodox Church rose from the ground in a heap of gray bricks and ornate stained-glass windows, making it feel much more welcoming than I thought possible. My eyes widened as I stepped out of the car, the streets lined with men in black suits and women adorned in every color but white. All of their heads were turned towards me as my feet ascended the steps and crossed the significant threshold of the church.

As I entered the building, hundreds of eyes pushed down on me like the weight of an entire city. Anyone who was anyone in New York was pressed into the orthodox church, all waiting to set their eyes on the long lost heir.

I swallowed, my feet stepping back but running into a muscular chest. "There's only one way out of here, Ana."

I nodded, taking the outstretched arm of Lev as the wedding march began and all of the guests stood to attention.

Their queen was about to be crowned.

I could see the back of Leo's head, his dark hair pushed back tastefully, and his broad shoulders stretching out his Armani suit like a second skin. I focused on him down the aisle and the man presenting me to him.

Everyone else in the room was here for the show, for the splendor of laying their eyes on the one and only Anastasia Romanov and watching her turn into a Solkov.

Be *welcomed* into the same family that ended hers.

What a spectacle I had allowed myself to become.

It wasn't until I was next to Leo that I noticed the man standing atop the daises.

"*Anazelina*, my child."

Father Grigori looked down on me; his thin lips pulled back in a way that was supposed to be welcoming but made my skin crawl. His milky eyes had always been able to piece through me in the most intrusive way, taking what I was unwilling to give.

"*Anastasia*," Leo said quietly.

I inhaled, turning to the man beside me and blinking slowly. Leo was handsome as always, but his warm voice wrapped me up and made it feel like I wasn't alone. His black eyes and olive skin entranced me and lured me into a false sense of security that I knew I would later regret, but it kept me afloat for now.

"Ah, yes. It will take time to get used to your new name, child." Father Grigori's eyes didn't waver from me as he clasped the worn bible in his hands. His long nails kept hold of the dark leather like it was a weapon.

For many, it was.

"What a blessing the lord has given you. Who could have ever known," His smile never reached his eyes, but I could feel him in my chest like a threat. Everything he ever did was with purpose - every word carefully chosen to inflict pain or coerce.

I lowered my head, an action ingrained into me since St. Basil's. "Father." I felt myself become nauseous, my body wavering even as Leo secured his hands in my own.

The ceremony continued, repeating Father Grigori when necessary and keeping our heads low. When it was time for the crowning, I looked towards the man on my left as we faced the audience of people witnessing a *lost* princess become a queen. The moment the golden crown hovered over me, the eyes of every man and woman lowered like they couldn't bear watching something so holy.

So *pure*.

The church was filled with people I'd never seen before; their black dress coats and jewel-encrusted bodies were all here for this. They wanted to bear witness to my parade. I wanted to look through their eyes momentarily and see what they saw. Would I look like the perfect princess they were hoping for, or would I still be the hollow hole of a woman I didn't recognize anymore?

The goblet of wine was shared between us, and Leo's dark gaze focused on me with an intensity I'd never been exposed to before. He looked down at me like I was his prize - no, his *salvation*.

He was still very much under the impression that he was about to launch a full-scale attack on the capital, using my name and blood as a means of control. Everything he did was about control, and isn't that what he used to ensnare me in the first place? He promised I could let go.

But now it was up to me to hold on. To pull my shit together and stop a war that would tear apart a family I didn't even know.

I turned back towards the man who put me in this situation, a severe look on his face that I couldn't begin to read. Father Grigori brought us a pillow holding two rings, both of which were made of gold, but the smaller of the two was etched in intricate vines. That would would be mine - my collar.

I wanted to drop everything and run, fuck the consequences, and get on a train to nowhere, but I knew I'd never make it down the aisle without a bullet in my back. Lev was right; there would only be one way out of this. I must have looked distressed because Leo squeezed my hand, which I had forgotten he was holding. I swallowed without looking at him, knowing his intensity would shake me even more.

When it came time to exchange the rings, I faced Leo but kept my gaze low; only when he started speaking did I peer up at him through my lashes. He spoke quietly and in our mother tongue. *"Ana, my light at the end of an unimaginable tunnel. I give you this ring as a symbol of my heart, my blood, my faith, and my protection. From this moment forward, you are mine, and I am yours - completely. I will spend the rest of my days as a shield against the world, a rock for you to sharpen yourself with, and a body for you to take comfort in. From this world and into the next, you will never be alone again."*

A lone tear fell from my eye before I finally took a breath, focusing on the warmth of my hand in his and holding on for dear life. It was hard not to think of this as real because a part of Leo *was* real. Deep down, I felt that a part of him could be the man he described, but I worried that Lev was right.

Leo had likely lost that part of him long ago, and in his place was a frightening beast that only I could stop. I wiped my tears away and tried to smile.

"Iz etogo mira v sleduyushchiy."

From this world and into the next.

Leo

She was unimaginable in that white dress, her auburn hair twisted below her lace veil and her plush lips shining with a gloss begging to be tasted. For a moment, I forgot who we were and where we were standing. The crowd of vultures was gone; I wasn't the vor of New York, and Ana's family would be in the front row - her sisters adorned in bridesmaids' dresses.

I could imagine another life where I met her on a park bench near 5th Avenue, a chocolate pastry in her petite hands and her flowing hair beneath an autumn cap. She would smile shyly at me as I passed, her hand covering her blush as I grinned and sat beside her. The weather would be gray, but the leaves would be a painting of red, orange, and yellow perfection. I'd ask her where she liked to go for coffee, and she'd laugh at my confidence but tell me anyway.

We'd go our separate ways after I complimented her crystal blue eyes, and then I'd be an hour early to the cafe the next day. She'd be twenty minutes early and giggle when she saw me waiting. We'd talk about literature and our careers; to which I'd be a lawyer, and she'd be a prima ballerina preparing for her first lead role.

We'd fall in love throughout the holidays and spend Christmas together in the church.

I would propose to her on a sunny day in June, our toes digging into the sand of a secluded beach where she'd say yes, and I'd make love to her as the sun fell into the ocean.

We would be *indescribably* happy.

But that isn't how the world works.

I was the *vor* of the Solkov Bratva - son of her family's murderer, and I had blackmailed Ana into marrying me so I could keep my throne.

I knew I wasn't the man she deserved, but she was the woman of my dreams and now *mine.*

My *Circe.*

My witchling.

S,o as I stood before the crowd of people who'd step over our dead bodies for a dollar, I promised her my body and soul.

It was the least I could do.

I turned to Ana when Father Grigori ended the crowning ceremony, bringing my hands to either side of her small face as she looked up at me with fear. It hurt me - how much she feared me. I leaned forward, lightly brushed my lips across hers, and whispered just loud enough for her to hear.

"You're radiant, my *wife.*"

She gasped against my lips, but all too soon, I was pulling away from her and turning back towards the jeering circus of rats and zealots.

Walking down the aisle with Ana on my right, I scanned the faces of every person in the crowd, their well-wishes and cheers muffled in my ears as we exited the church. Lev was following behind us through the doors, his voice raising as people tried to speak with Ana - the long lost *printcessa* of the Romanov dynasty.

"Anastasia! Anastasia, were you really at St.Basil's this entire time?"

"Anastasia, have you seen Alexei yet?"

"Ana-".

I had kept a careful eye on Lev and Ana the last few days, unsure of my brother's warmth towards her. He had never been a man of conviction, and it worried me how close they had become. I trusted

Lev, but I didn't trust him not to be sucked in by her broken spirit and apparent addiction. I knew he would fall into her capable hands if he could see a reflection of himself in her. Because no matter how broken Ana appeared, I knew she was masterful in manipulation.

It might already be too late, so I fretted over what I was to do with my most loyal soldier.

My blood.

My gaze caught the round face of John Davis; his blonde hair slicked back while his pill-popping wife held onto his elbow with a fierce determination. She looked entirely out of place among the vor wives because they were predators, and Elisabeth Davis could smell a threat from a mile away. I nodded towards him once, and he waved an uneasy hand my way before we stepped out of the church.

The car door slammed, and we drove off towards Brooklyn. Ana sat beside me in her silk gown, eyes focused on her fingers twirling in her lap. The snow was coming down outside, and the skies were a dark gray against the city lights.

"Moy zhena," I said while placing my hand in hers. She froze at my touch, making me curse under my breath. I'd flinch away from my touch if I were her, so I pulled my hand from hers and let her sit in silence.

I could feel her leg bouncing, her eyes darting out the window, and her fingers poking around her mouth as she chewed her nails off. She was a caged bird.

As we pulled outside the house on Cobble Hill, I grabbed Ana's arm before she could step out. *"Lisichka -".*

"Just fucking stop it," Ana cursed as her head swivelled to me, and her eyes were rimmed in tears. "It's over with. Can't you leave me alone now?"

I sighed, dropping her hand and moving away from her. "It'll never be over, Circe. You're mine now, from this life until the next. This marriage might have been born out of lies, but I don't break a vow once made."

She frowned. *"Hateful to me as the gates of Hades is that man who hides one thing in his heart and speaks another."*

I winced, knowing this would be a long road to gain her trust. She was a creature who held herself closed tight; I couldn't tell what parts were because of me and what was just her shitty life. She'd been a survivor up until now, but I wanted to make her a goddess. I wanted her to feel like I felt about her, but I couldn't force that.

She'd have to choose it.

Slowly turned to me and whispered, "So Alexei is safe now? The crimson crosses have been resent?"

I nodded. "All six families have taken back their crosses out of respect to their *vor's* new family. A wedding gift."

Before I could even tell what was happening, her hand lashed out and struck me across my cheek with more force than I thought she was capable of.

"That's for not telling me about the seventh seat," she hissed at me

I was too shocked to do anything as she climbed out of the car, and I watched her stomp through my line of soldiers, who all took a healthy step away from her as she passed. She spun around once she got to the door, gave me a bright smile, and then promptly raised her middle finger high in the air towards me and disappeared into the house.

Once my surprise wore off, I jumped out of the door and slammed through the front door. Ana swirled around in her silk dress, eyes bright with fury as she stomped down the hallway towards the kitchen, passing housekeepers and cooks who gave her a wide birth.

I growled. "You're all done for today. Get. Out."

All of their heads bowed as they passed through the front door, their heels filling the silence that I intended to replace with my wife's screams.

Locking the door behind them, I followed Ana into the kitchen, where she was tossing her heels into the corner, ripping her veil off, and frantically trying to do the same to her wedding ring.

"Such a fucking brat, even on your wedding day."

Her red hair spun around her in auburn curtains, hanging around her face as her eyes locked with mine, and I swore she was trying to set me on fire. Her chest heaved, pushing against the thin silk that wrapped around her so deliciously.

"Go fuck yourself," she said with a devious smile.

I hummed. "Oh, Circe, that was quite a show you put on out there. I hope you understand that I can't let that go unpunished."

"This was never about saving Alexei. You just wanted to take back D.C., and you knew I'd agree to anything once I realised I had a family out there."

Fucking Lev.

I sighed, "That's just a part of it."

"Your empty words are *evil*." Angry tears fell from her eyes, and I stepped towards her. Her back was to the kitchen counters, hands splayed out wide behind her as she shook her head. "I knew it was for the seventh seat before I walked down that aisle, but to hear your lies about being *my rock* and *protecting me?* You're vile, Leoniv Solkov."

A sharp pain punctured my chest, right where a heart should lay. "I meant every word I said to you before God. You are a bright light in this dark world that we were both born into. I want to break the cycle of sins being handed down from father to child -."

"Then make sure Alexei takes his seat and rules it from Chicago." She stood up straight, her nose in the air as she spoke of things she knew nothing about. She took a breath, stepping away from the counter and towards me. "If you want me to stop fighting you, you'll ensure that Alexei takes the Romanov seat and D.C. is left standing."

My lips rose, and I leaned towards the red witch who was playing a dangerous game. "And what makes you think I want you to stop fighting me, *Circe*?"

I could see her visibly swallow.

Ana's plush lips parted, her bright eyes wide, and I couldn't help but think of what she looked like with makeup running down her face and cheeks hollow as she sucked my cock.

"I told you that you could keep all of this up, fighting me and being a fucking brat, but that you would repay in kind behind closed doors." I was so close to her now that as her chest rose and fell, I could feel her hard nipples pressing against my chest.

I groaned as my hand came to rest on her waist, her eyes hooded as she fought her instincts to run and hide from me - to flee instead of surrender. I leaned down so that my lips grazed the flesh of her cheeks that were still damp with tears. "I want your fire, *Lisichka.* In fact, I crave it like a man who hasn't felt the sun's warmth in millennia."

She whimpered, her hands coming to rest against my chest, but she didn't push me away.

Thank God she didn't push me away.

Ana

I couldn't think with his arms wrapped around my waist and his lips whispering sweet threats into my ear. I'd planned to forget everything he and I had settled on days ago and say a big fuck you to ever willingly being with him again. But the way he made my heart skip a beat and my skin flush with heat . . . I worried I wasn't strong enough to fight him.

To fight my husband.

"I have never looked at something more holy than you with that golden crown on your head. My eyes have yet to witness a divine sight as my wife wrapped in white silk, shaking in our kitchen as I prepare to bring her sweet release."

I audibly moaned, my thighs clenching together as his strong hands squeezed my ass, and he chuckled. "Do you want release, *Circe*? Do you want to come on my fingers right here in our kitchen?"

Is that what I wanted?

His fingers moved around me, digging hard into my ass before lifting me off the ground and setting me on the cold granite counter. He was nestled between my open legs, now eye level with me. Leo's eyes still held a bright fire, but he seemed more serious as he took a breath.

"I don't want to keep things from you, *Lisichka*, but there are some parts of my empire that I'd rather leave outside of our marriage."

My arms were resting on his chest still, and a feeling of warmth settled below my touch. "I don't like being lied to, Leo."

I didn't want to be left in the dark, knowing that the shadows were where the beast with the sharpest teeth hid away. He tried to keep me shielded from those things, but there was no such thing as safety in a city run by the Solkovs.

He shook his head. "I'm not going to lie, but I might not share everything with you. I told you I was out of town for business, and it's true. But, you don't need to know what that business was."

My brow raised. "So it had something to do with D.C?"

"Don't ask me about my business, *Lisichka.*"

My jaw tightened, hands balling into fists against his tuxedo. "The moment you put that ring on my finger, it became *our* business. Husband," I added for good measure.

He wanted to use my name and my dead family as a way to grow his empire, but I wouldn't roll over like a dog. If he really thought I would turn my head into the satin sheets and close my eyes, he was wrong. Lev had told me not to let his brother bring me down into the darkness with him, but what if it was the only way to come out alive?

Leo placed both hands on the counter and straightened his back, looking down at me again with dark, discerning eyes. His brows rose for a moment before he chuckled. "I thought you'd prefer to stay locked away in the library for the rest of your life, but instead, you wish to dive into the pit of rats and vultures?"

I huffed. "And what made you think I'd want to hide away?"

"Because it's what I would have preferred for myself - if given the choice."

I frowned, taken back by that answer but not entirely surprised. He'd told me his father would drag him from his books, putting a knife in his hand and forcing a boy to become a man.

"It's like you said, Leo, neither of us ever had a choice in this life. The moment I was born into the Romanov family, I was destined to be a bratva wife. Wasn't I?"

Leo's face was severe, dark eyes staring down at me as my back bent over the countertops. His hands moved to rest against my waist, and he leaned in to whisper in my ear. "I think you were always destined to be *my* wife."

My heart leapt into my throat as his hands continued to move up my body, circling me and caging our chests against one another. His lips were curled, and I could feel his breath on my cheeks. Suddenly, he lifted me onto the counter, sitting between my open thighs.

"I'm going to fuck you now, witchling. I'll take you right here in our kitchen, and then you'll come with me to our room, where you'll kneel for me like the obedient little wife you are."

I couldn't help the whimper that escaped from my lips as he ground forward into my aching center, his hands digging into my waist until it hurt. Leo was enjoying this power play, and I couldn't lie that it was exactly what I needed. I didn't have to love or care for the man to be pleased. Like he said, I could defy him outside of sex.

I wasn't losing, just negotiating for peace.

I obediently opened my legs wider for him, allowing my eyes to shudder when his warm hands landed on my thighs and spread heat across my skin. Leo's dark gaze was watching me with a lust that only a crazed man could express - a lion staring down a lifetime of prey that would sit pretty and let him devour it whole.

I was that prey right now, and I was very much willing to be his supper, spread wide for him to taste and enjoy.

"Do you want me to taste that pretty pussy of yours, Ana?" His fingers trailed up my legs until they reached the lacy lingerie Ambre had forced me into.

I bucked my hips in response to him, but he tutted me. "Ah, ah, ah. Use your words, witchling."

"Please," I begged the most sexy and vile man in New York. A man with the blood of god knows how many people are on his hands—my husband.

He hummed, hooking his fingers into my panties and, pulling them down my legs and tucking them into his pocket. "I still need you to tell me what you want, Ana. This relationship only works if you communicate with me."

I wanted to be frustrated with him, but I also knew that this was likely the one aspect of our arrangement I would have a voice in. I could tell him to stop, and a part of me knew that he would without question.

That was powerful.

I peered at him through my lashes, eyes hooded with lust as he started to loosen his tie. "I want you to lick my cunt until I scream your name, and then I want you to fuck me without remorse. I want you to tie my hands and fuck me while I scream, husband."

In an instant, Leo had my legs in both hands, spreading me wide on the kitchen counter as a wolfish grin spread across his devilish features. His eyes were clouded in need, and his tongue ran across his bottom lip as he stared at me.

"My darling, Circe. My wicked witchling. I'm going to enjoy hearing you scream for me."

And scream, I did. The moment his tongue lashed out across my throbbing clit, my head fell back in ecstasy. Leo was determined, unyielding and fucking sexy as he moaned into my heat - his tongue swirling around my cunt as my hands laced through his silky hair. His hands were holding me in place, forcing my knees apart so that he had unlimited access to the splendour of his wife.

"Fuck, Leo." I groaned wantonly as the stubble along his cheeks teased the delicate inner parts of my thighs. It was an experience to have a deadly and powerful man between your thighs, exploring and ravishing you as you scream his name.

My fingers dug into his scalp, forcing him closer to me while he moaned. "Don't rush me through this, witchling. I like to enjoy my dessert."

With one long, slow lick up my center, I felt my stomach build with desire. My eyes started to roll to the back of my head as Leo pushed me further and further towards the edge of completion. I stared up at the ornate ceiling, my mouth agape as the vor of New York plunged his tongue into my wet pussy, and I came all over his appreciative lips. My legs shook in his hold, my heart racing as he lapped and nuzzled further into my centre.

"Leo!" I screamed into the quiet house as he chuckled between my thighs. His fingers worked to massage my quivering legs as I caught my breath.

Finally, when my body gave out, he stood and wrapped a strong arm around my waist before smashing his slick lips into mine. I could taste myself on his tongue, sweet and musky, while he moaned against me. You could have told me that Leo hung the very stars in the sky, and at that moment, I would have believed you.

His hands rested underneath my arse, and I wrapped my legs around Leo's hard waist while he picked me up from the counter. He didn't break out of the kiss, his tongue exploring my mouth greedily while intermittently nipping at my bottom lip until I groaned. I could feel them swelling from the punishment of his kiss, and yet I knew there was still so much more to come.

Leo tore his mouth away from me only to hurry us up the stairs, walking me to the first room he'd taken me to the night he pushed me over the edge of temptation. He all but threw me down onto the bed, my ass bouncing against the mattress as Leo ripped his shirt open and lunged for me again.

His mouth was on mine, hands tangled in my hair as it assaulted my senses. His warm body was flush against mine, fingers pulling and kneading at my body while his lips and tongue did all of the talking. I could feel his cock pressed into me, hard and ready for the task.

Leo tore away from me and grinned wickedly. "Hands above your head, witchling."

I did as I was told, raising my arms and smiling when he wrapped a silk cord around my wrists. I was staring up at him while he did this, memorised by the curve of his jaw and the rich colour of his brown eyes that made me feel alight with need. I pushed away all of my other thoughts concerning who this man was outside the bedroom.

That was an issue for tomorrow, Ana.

Once Leo had secured my bindings, the feeling of soft silk digging into my sensitive skin drove me insane; he smiled down at me and ran his hands over my breasts that were still contained in my dress.

"I want to tear this off of you with my teeth, wife. I think I'll keep it and make you wear it whenever you're acting up. Maybe that will be a fine form of punishment, pleasing me on your knees while I call you *my bride.*"

I nodded my head, and my breath escalated like an animal in heat while Leo dipped his fingers under the collar of my dress - his warm skin brushing against the tops of my breasts. His thighs were on either side of me, half holding me in place and half driving me into the mattress below.

"I want you to beg me, little fox. My *Lisichka,*" he cooed down at me as he drove his hardened cock across my bare pussy. The friction from his pants made me squirm, and the pinch of his belt hurt in the most delicious way.

"Please, Leo."

He drove forward again, pushing my body halfway across the bed as I cried out from the sensation. My clit was swollen, well abused by his tongue lashing and now being forced to submit under the weight of his leather belt. "You're in my kingdom now, *Lisichka.* Here in this room, behind that wooden door, you call me sir."

I was breathing heavily, and I nodded as his eyes gleamed. "Please, sir. I want you to fuck me."

"Good girl," he cooed as he sat up. I was staring at where his tattoos peaked from behind his half-opened shirt, dark ink in the old language. When he pulled the rest of his shirt off and threw it to the floor, I licked my lips at the sight of him above me.

Leo knew the sort of lust he provoked - the wanton need for him to fuck me until I couldn't breathe. It was about power here, and I was willing to give it to him.

Only here.

Leo pulled the hem of my dress up, exposing myself to him as he smiled appreciatively. He kept his eyes trained on me while unbuckling his pants and reaching in to grasp his cock. "I've been dreaming about your tight little pussy since the day you crawled out of my bed. Every night I lay awake, fisting my cock and thinking about retaking you."

I bucked upwards, my hips yearning to feel his collide with mine in a symphony of flesh and beautiful moans. I'd been thinking of him too, and the ache I'd felt for days after he fucked me senseless and held me close. I sat in that library for hours with a phantom ache between my legs.

I sighed, my chest heaving with adrenaline and anticipation. "Please, sir. I need to feel you inside of me."

He nodded, pulling his cock out of his pants finally and stroking it over my body as he watched me wiggle and beg for him. Leo Solkov liked to watch me beg, and I could tell it was something he intended on making me do quite often now that I was legally his.

Leo leaned forward, quickly brushing the tip of his cock through my slit teasingly. I huffed, lifting to try and entice him to take me fully. To just fuck me already!

It must have been the look on my face or the way I pleaded with my eyes that he finally decided to put me out of my misery. In one quick thrust, Leo had impaled me to the hilt.

"Argh!" I cried out as he fucked me long and hard, his body propped up on his elbows while he grabbed my bound hands and tugged the rope harder.

His hips against mine were unyielding, strong and furious like the waves of a hurricane against the seawall. He would pull out to the tip, his lips curling, and then push back into me until I felt like I was going to be broken in two.

I wanted him to fuck me in half.

Fuck me into pieces and glue me back together with his sweat and moans, stitching me back up with his tongue and covering me in his come like the filthy slut I was. I needed to have every part of him and feel like he could have every part of me. I would give him anything at this moment if he asked. It was a hazardous situation for me to find myself in, but I also knew that with my pussy wrapped around his cock he would give me the world if I asked.

"Fuck, Ana," he groaned as his eyes closed in pleasure.

Leo sat up, pulling my legs up until my knees were against my chest and then continued to drive into me with a mind-altering force. I didn't think he could get any deeper, but he did!

"Please," I moaned as my breath was taken away. I didn't know what I was begging for, but I was. Each thrust of his cock was a punch to the gut, and his words were a salve.

"Your tight cunt is so perfect."

Thrust.

"Do you like the way I can make you fall apart on my cock?"

Thrust.

"Come for me, baby."

And I did.

"Leo!"

My pussy tightened around him, squeezing him until he groaned out my name and came with a roar. *"Lisichka!"*

Leo's cock throbbed inside of me, my walls still pulsing with every beat of my heart and milking his dick for everything it was worth. It was times like this that I was appreciative of my IUD because when Leo pulled out of me, I could feel his cum sliding down my cunt and soaking the sheets between us.

He reached forward, wiping his cum off of my thigh and then thrusting his wet fingers back into my pussy with a satisfied smirk on his face. "Fuck the wedding dress, I'd rather see you covered in my cum."

I was still out of breath, and all I could do was muster up a weak groan as my thighs quivered with exhaustion.

Leo stood from the bed, wiping sweat from his brows before walking off to the bathroom and giving me a great view of his taunt ass. My hands were still bound above me, but I was too tired to care. I thought about getting up to join him, moving my legs and feeling the cum still pooling out of me, but then my eyes started to droop.

Before long, I was dozing off in my husband's bed - bound, fucked and covered in his cum without another care in the world.

Leo

My fingers dipped below the satin knot that held her hands in place, pulling on it gently so she didn't wake. Her beautiful, auburn hair was splayed across the evergreen sheets, and her dress was still around her waist. I let myself stand over in her admiration, wanting to commit every curve and freckle to memory so I could paint a picture of them.

I left Ana in my bed, heading downstairs to tuck into my office and think about how I would deal with the fallout of this union. Lev had been unable to keep his fucking mouth shut, so now my wife was fully aware of the stakes. The nation's capital was a powerful city to hold, with easy access to politicians from across the country who could be paid a hefty sum to turn a blind eye to their docks.

I'd held New York for years, and I was never going to give it up while there was air in my lungs - even after, it would be my heir who controlled the city and all its wealth. An heir that I hoped Ana would give me soon and solidify my ownership of the city to even the most staunch Romanov supporters. A wedding ring on Anastasia's hand was one thing, but a blood heir would be welcomed into the church and every home this side of the Atlantic.

Shipments of weapons were already arriving in port with direct orders to check the boxes and then nail them shut again. I'd have to arrange transport from here to DC without using the coast. The

Lucchesse would have their eyes on every ship and every parcel that entered that city.

Weapons and firepower aside, my biggest concern was of a blonde-haired young man with a thirst for Solkov blood. The bleeding crosses had been sent back, but could I hold off the other families if more bodies started to appear in Chicago? What about here in this very city?

I bent over my computer desk, pulling up layouts of back roads down the East Coast and communications channels to watch from the West when my bastardy little brother walked through the door.

"Where have you been?" I asked him without glancing up from my maps. I needed to get these routes out to my men and have sweeps of the outer neighbourhoods near Little Italy checked for new faces. Alexei was likely already in the city, and I knew Ana's face on the cover of the Times in her wedding dress would ruffle some feathers.

I heard Lev take an ungraceful fall into the chairs across from my desk, his loud sigh permeating the room and making me look up. My brother was still dressed in his wedding clothes, though his jacket was gone, and the expensive shirt around his shoulders was wrinkled as if he'd slept in it.

He stared back at me, eyes rimmed in red from recent drug use, and he looked more tired than he had this morning. "What is it?" I pushed aside my things and leaned over the table towards him. "Inhale your last stash of snow?" My patience with my brother had grown threadbare, and with each look at Ana, I was sure there would be holes before long.

Lev was slumped across the leather upholstery half-haphazardly, head lulled to the side as he looked at me with eyes that were glazed over. "You're not going to let Alexei take that seat."

I blinked at him. "Is that really what this is all about? You're the one who told me it wouldn't be a good idea to let a Romanov anywhere near the council."

He scoffed, rubbing at his face while his legs bounced irritably. My brother's drug use had gotten worse over the years, falling in and out of being functional and dipping towards suicide on the darkest of occasions. I knew why he did it. It was a lot easier to bust someone's face in and take lives when you're high off your ass.

It was an escape from his reality - a reality that I upheld.

"You know," he said before straightening. "I thought it couldn't get any worse than what Dad did. I told myself this was much better than digging two more graves, but I'm not so sure anymore."

My jaw tightened, and I had to keep myself from jumping over the table and beating some sense into the kid. He knew why I decided - we decided to approach the situation this way. A marriage would strengthen our family's connection to the city and keep Alexei out of our hair. It was also a gift to allow the young Romanov heir to live when many others in my position would not.

"What would you have me do, hm? Let's switch chairs, and you tell me how to run this fucking family and keep our throne."

"It's your throne," he hissed at me.

"You're a Solkov - it's our throne."

He sneered at me, looking around the room while his leg continued to bounce and bounce and -.

"Can you sit fucking still for five minutes," I snapped.

An ugly frown covered his face, and he looked over his shoulder briefly before scooting closer. "What are you going to do with that poor girl upstairs?"

"That poor girl is my *wife*. I'll do whatever I damn well please."

Quickly, his hand shot out and slammed down on my desk, a rare outburst of anger that Lev had never used against me before. I looked up at him in shock but also in warning. He might be my brother, but he was also my soldier.

He pointed a shaking finger at me. "You're going to ruin her, just like Dad ruined us."

"Ana will not be a part of the business -."

"But isn't she?" He interrupted me. "Your entire marriage is one big business deal, but it only favours one side! You basically put a gun to her brother's head and told her she had a choice between Alexei's blood on that marriage contract or her signature."

I stood up, my chair slamming against the back wall as I walked around the desk towards Lev. The man stood his ground, looking almost eye level with me as I stepped into his personal space. "Do we have a problem? Have I allowed you to become too attached to Ana over secret bottles of vodka and weed?" His face fell, and his eyes grew wide while I nodded. "Yeah, of course I knew about that."

Lev at least had the better sense of looking guilty, diverting his eyes. "She's fighting an addiction; I couldn't let her just stop. She's already so thin and weak. I was worried she'd become sick if she went cold turkey."

"I know that I really do, and it's why I didn't step in and stop you. But I won't allow my blood to switch sides just because a beautiful woman listened to him play on his precious piano and smiled at him."

He scoffed, and I reached out to grab his wrinkled shirt in my fists. "I've let you get close to Ana because she's more likely to listen if she doesn't feel alone. I didn't think I'd need to worry about an orphan girl manipulating my best soldier."

His face became enraged, and he pushed against me, making me stumble back as he took a step away from me. "I'm your *brother*! I'm not a gruntwork immigrant from the motherland who needs a warm meal! This was supposed to be a family!"

"This is a business!" I shouted back at him, my shoulders tense as I prepared myself for him to attack me. When he was using, Lev was unpredictable. "You never wanted more responsibility, and I was okay with that. You handled personal affairs and logistics because that's. What. You. Wanted."

Ana

When I woke up, it was utterly dark, and after spreading my arms out across the satin sheets, it was apparent to me that I was alone, and it was likely that Leo never came back to bed. I pushed myself up on my elbows, stretching out my legs and groaning at the dull ache in my thighs. God, that had all really happened.

I'd told myself that I wouldn't feel guilty about it because it was, after all, just an agreement in the bedroom, but there wasn't a way that this wouldn't spill over into every day. Could I allow myself to let go and give over control while on my knees but not bend under his gaze while vertical?

I padded into the joint bathroom, blinking against the white light that illuminated the white walls, white floors and even whiter countertops. In every direction, there was pale marble and wide mirrors that made it impossible not to see myself cloaked in my rumpled wedding dress.

My hair swung around me in a red veil, clinging to my neck and sticking out in all directions from spending far too much time with the back of my head against a bed and getting fucked. I took the time to peel myself from my dress, letting it fall onto the perfect floor and then staring at myself in the mirrors.

I felt different.

Looking down at the simple gold band on my finger, I remembered that the engagement ring was still untouched in the library. It wasn't used in an orthodox wedding, and a part of me preferred the gold ring. It was small, unsuspecting and quiet. It was a fox hiding in the brush and waiting for the kill.

My eyes lingered over the rest of myself, though, and I swallowed. I'd gained weight in the past week, even though I ate at irregular times and was still abusing alcohol. The pantry had been packed with snacks, the freezer with ready-made meals, and I devoured them between bouts of Leo or Lev stomping through the bottom story.

My hair looked shinier; getting washed regularly and brushed meant I appeared like a normal human being, not the homeless trash I'd been for years. It had been hard to care about my looks when I was hungry.

Stepping into Leo's shower, I avoided his body wash, already having made myself too comfortable with my new husband. I rinsed, avoiding my hair and quickly got out before wrapping the towel around my body and padding back into the room. The screen on Leo's bedside table said it was nearly eleven at night, and my stomach growled as if it'd forgotten I hadn't eaten at all today. I was too nervous this morning to allow Lev to force toast in my mouth.

I opened the door into the hall and hurried back to my room, closing it with a quiet click before dressing myself in simple leggings and a sweater that didn't look too warm for the house.

There were small bags of chips, cookies and granola bars that I'd stashed in the dresser for when I wanted to avoid humans, but I knew there were pyrizhky that the cook had filled the freezer with and just needed to be baked. The thought of a warm puff pastry filled with meats and cabbage made my mouth salivate so I could dare the risk of running into anyone.

It was late, after all.

Down the hall, Lev's door was closed, and I cocked my head, wondering where he could have gone. He'd always left the door ajar in case I needed anything, and there was no soft lull of music coming from behind the door.

I managed to get into the kitchen, my hands on the oven timer before the lights flickered on, and I winced against the bright assault. "I thought you'd sleep until morning," Leo said with amusement as I turned to see him near the hallway that led towards his office.

Always working.

He wore grey sweatpants that hung low on his hips and a matching t-shirt that road up his abs as he leaned against the door frame. I could see the peak of his tattoos across his lower V-line, and I wet my lips.

"I worked up an appetite," I responded with a grin but then frowned when I caught myself. Out here, I was supposed to hate his guts still.

He snorted, walking into the kitchen and peeking over my shoulder at the frozen pyrizhky I'd placed into a pan. "Yulia is a woman of great talents; if she were my age, I probably would have married her after tasting her solyanka."

"What a shame you've been saddled with an orphan who never learned to cook."

He raised a brow at me. "Yulia can teach you; she'll be here tomorrow."

I put the dish into the oven and then skirted away from him, biting my tongue as he eyed me. "Because that's what wives do, right?" I said under my breath, but it was loud enough for him to hear me.

"You don't have to, but I thought it could be something you could do with all your time. There are only so many books I can fit in the library," he tried to lighten the mood, but it didn't work. I know that he'd meant it in a helpful way, I really did, but all I could hear was Lev reminding me that I was supposed to pump out an heir for the Solkov bratva. Be the dutiful Russian wife and make solyanka for my husband to come home to after a long day of killing people and bribing politicians.

"And if I want to do something else," I said while pulling wine out of the refrigerator, noticing how his gaze dropped to the bottle in my hand. "What if I want to work?"

"I can find charities you could volunteer for around New York. Or even work with the church, just not with Father Grigori," he said firmly.

I shivered because the thought of being alone with that man made my skin crawl. He'd always been a shadow in my youth, lurking around corners and nudging me away from the other priests. When I was a teen, I thought maybe it was because the church had predators, and he was trying to protect me, but I soon found out that he was a wolf in sheep's clothing.

I sighed. "I mean an actual job, Leo." I was pulling drawers out, looking for the corkscrew so I could drown my shame in alcohol.

"No," he shook his head. "It wouldn't be right considering your station."

I laughed. "My station? Are you serious?"

"Ana, you're now a very wealthy woman. There's no need for you to work or worry about finances. I've already had a bank account set up for you with a weekly -."

I turned around with a fury. "If you say *allowance*, I'll stab you with a kitchen knife."

He took a breath, raising his hands like he was trying to calm an angry animal. I huffed, turning back around in search of the damned wine opener. This kitchen was too big. How many drawers could there be?

"It wouldn't look right for you to work, and besides, the security risk isn't worth it. Many people out there'd like to get their hands on the most priceless bargaining chip on the East Coast."

I slammed a drawer shut in exhaustion. "So I can volunteer at a bratva-backed charity for the rest of my days under the watchful eyes of your *byki*?" I shook my head, marching around Leo and shouldering him out of the way as I tried and failed to find something to open the fucking bottle. "I don't think so."

Leo watched me, stepping aside as I tore the kitchen apart. His arms were crossed over his chest, and a heavy line of aggravation settled on his brow - as usual when we were arguing.

Married life.

"Bratva wives do not work, Ana. Your mother ran several charitable foundations in her spare time while raising you all, and plenty of other wives would be more than happy to bring you along while you decide on a charity of choice."

My body chilled, and I thought of a lovely laugh that had haunted me my entire life like a taunt. A picture of a world that I could have lived in, but still, if I was always a bratva daughter, then this was my destiny. It just happened differently.

All roads lead to Rome.

"Well, the youngest daughter didn't grow old enough to learn about her *duties.* I was raised by cruel nuns who told me the only way to get a warm meal was to work. It looks like you ended up with the wrong Romanov daughter."

Leo rolled his eyes and muttered under his breath. *"Polnaya protivopolozhnost' Ol'ge."*

I blinked. Olga?

He looked away from me, and I marched forward and grabbed his chin between my thin fingers, though he stared at the wall. "Look at me," I demanded the man who now ruled my life. "Why do you keep mentioning Olga?"

His body was rigid, muscles tight as he turned his head to look me in the eyes. Leo seemed tense, and a sad look washed over his sharp features.

"How well did you know my family?"

"Well enough."

My fingers dug into his chin, which was still in my grasp. "How. Well."

He tore his head away from me and took two giant steps back; his footsteps echoed in the empty house. I'd never seen such anguish on a man, his head a battleground for words he wanted to share and memories he wished would blow away like snow in the wind.

When he finally spoke, his hands balled into fists at his side; he was quiet. "I was betrothed to Olga from the age of fourteen, our parents thinking that her quiet demeanour would do well with my own. She also enjoyed reading and wouldn't be seen without a book tucked under her arm at every party. It seems you got much more of your father's temper," he said while rubbing his face.

I sat frozen in silence as he walked around the kitchen and fell into one of the chairs that backed into the breakfast nook.

"I hadn't spent too much time with her, your mother always hiding behind every bookshelf in your manor as we read silently together. She was a beautiful girl, with strawberry hair and brown eyes that always looked too big for her small face."

He sighed, looking at me with a grim expression. "Maybe it was a blessing that I hadn't gotten to know her better. It certainly made the events that happened two years later a little easier."

My hands were held tight against my chest, emotions caught in my throat as he spoke about a young girl that I couldn't even remember. I tried thinking back to the photo of us, but even that memory was clouded.

He turned around and leaned back against the far wall, his dark demeanour a stark contrast to the egg-white panelling of the kitchen.

"My father didn't tell Lev or me what he was planning until the first gunshots rang out, and your father was announced dead to the entirety of the brotherhood. *The tyrant of New York is dead*; he had shouted to the ballroom full of families and guests. No one there was shocked that Vlad Solkov could or would do something so bold and gruesome," he said. Leo looked up at me as his face contorted, "But I was. She was supposed to be my wife. I had always known my father was a monster, but that night, it was like standing next to the devil at the gates of Hades."

"He put a bullet in her head and announced it to the entire party," I whispered in disgust.

He shook his head. "No, he announced the death of Nicholas, but he just let everyone rightfully assume that the entire family had been taken care of, too. But we all knew what he meant. We all knew he had killed his own son's betrothed."

I felt pain for Leo, knowing that the loss of a family I didn't realise was tricky but nothing compared to if I actually could remember them. I had always considered Leo and Lev accomplices in the story, but he was only sixteen.

"But how did we get away? Who spared Alexei and I?"

Who would have taken such a risk, knowing what kind of man Vlad Solkov was?

Leo's shoulders sagged, head falling forward so that his hair fell into his eyes in dark curtains. "I couldn't save Olga, but I could get out the youngest." His head raised, eyes trained on me as he said quietly, "You were *so* small. Your red hair was caked in enough blood that I wasn't sure you would even make it."

I moved around the kitchen until my back was to the door, separating my husband and me. "You're telling me that you're the one who left me at St. Basil's?"

My body shook, eyes darting from his worried face to the hallway. Another piece of my life has been thrown carelessly in front of me, and I couldn't keep track of my racing thoughts.

Why was I left at St. Basil's and Alexei sent away?

Does Lev know that it was his brother who saved us?

What would happen if the other Brotherhood members knew what Leo did?

"I didn't drop you physically at the door but took you from the basement. You were a pile of tulle, thrown over Alexei like a shield. You girls had always been so protective of him," he admitted. "I was only sixteen, and you were turning ten, yet our lives had been changed forever that night, and I couldn't take any of it back. I couldn't stop the machine that had already been started."

My nose filled with the damp smell of a cellar and the burnt residue that accompanied sparklers.

Or gunshots.

"Then what," I asked quietly.

His hands pushed through his hair, grabbing at it before sighing loudly. "Then I handed you to someone I thought I could trust, and over a decade later, I got word that a red-haired beauty was selling drugs in Brooklyn."

"How?"

He laughed softly. "How could I not? You look more like your mother than any of the girls, and the golden talisman around your neck told me you were Grigori's. The same man I handed you over to. I knew immediately that it was you, and I would brush it all under the rug until Alexei made his move in Chicago. I was going just to let it go, Ana."

I gasped. Father Grigori had known who I was the entire time and never said a word to me. He had let me feel alone and trapped in that orphanage when I had a brother and a birthright just down the Hudson.

That's why he had told me to stay away from the bratva . . .

"How gracious of you," I spit at him. "To have handed me over to the church."

"What else should I have done?" He pushed his chair away, walking towards me as I backed out of the kitchen. "Should I have let my father finish the job a decade ago? How about letting the other families take revenge on your brother, who's barely a man? Maybe I should have put a bullet in his head and spared me the fucking trouble of arguing with you about -."

I growled lowly, "You should have told me about the fucking seat!"

"You aren't eligible for it anyway!"

"And the Lucchese family - do they get a say on what happens to their city? Your father abandoned it for New York, and now they're to be punished for it, too?" I crossed my arms as his face dropped, shock dancing across his sharp features.

His voice was low in warning. "You don't have any idea what's happening in D.C, and the fact that Lev is talking to you about it means that I have even more to worry about."

"Don't blame him for telling me the truth when you refused. He has been the only one to ask me what I wanted in all this."

He stepped closer, and I tried to back away, but when I hit the wall, he was able to cage me in. "And what is it, dear wife, that you're hoping to get out of all of this? What secrets can I tell you that would ease your pretty head at night?"

"Fuck you."

He snorted, "I already get to."

My hand shot up to slap the smirk off his face, but he caught it and held it between us—the evidence of my outburst.

He tilted his head, "You didn't think I'd let you do that twice, did you?"

"A girl can dream."

"You're a fucking brat."

"And you are a *monster*!"

I didn't have time to breathe as his lips smashed into mine, stealing away my venomous words and dangerous ideas. My fists hammered into his chest, trying to push him away even though I wanted nothing more than to melt into his arms and forget about the outside world. I wanted to live an eternity in those green silk sheets.

But that was his way of controlling me. It was his leverage. I finally mustered enough strength to shove him away, breaking our kiss and gasping for air.

"You want this just as much as I do," he growled while trying to walk towards me again.

"No," I cried as tears sprung from my eyes. "I hate you!"

Ana

I tore through the house, running up the polished stairs - my legs shaking as I raced down the long haul towards Lev's room.

Pushing through the closed door without a backward glance, my eyes landed on the piano bench, lightly illuminated by the lamp in the corner of the room.

My hands gently passed over the leather before pushing it upward, looking for the bottle of vodka that I knew Lev kept stashed in here. I pushed past pill bottles and bags full of weed and coke before finally grabbing a hold of the glass container and smiling triumphantly.

That smile faded as the door creaked behind me, and a heavy footstep entered the room. "Are you trying to get me killed?"

Without turning around, I unscrewed the cap and brought the bottle to my lips. "We're already dead inside Lev. Anyone attached to this fucking city has given up their soul to be here, and I just signed mine over to the devil himself."

Lev reached forward and uncharacteristically tore the liqueur from my hands.

"Hey!" I shouted as I turned to see him staring down at me with a twisted face. His clothes were rumpled, and he'd obviously been using today. Lev's undereyes were cast in dark shadows, and his face looked pale and sallow.

"You can't just come in here and drown yourself in fucking vodka.

Have you talked to Leo about Alexie's seat?" Lev put the bottle on the side table, and my eyes followed it.

I sighed. "I'm tired, Lev. In case you don't remember, I had a traumatising day of being married off to New York's best-dressed serial killer and drug lord."

He snorted, his red-rimmed eyes bouncing around the room. "Traumatizing enough for you to spread your legs the moment you got home?"

I stumbled back as if shot. "What the fuck?"

He let out an angry snarl, "I'm turning on my own brother for you, and you can't get out of your fucking head!"

"No one asked you to *turn* on your brother. If anything, you're the one who keeps saying that I need to do something to keep him out of D.C.!"

Lev moved forward, his finger pointed in my face, and I could smell the whiskey on his breath. He was mixing an upper with downers, and that was never good. "You walked into that church so sure of yourself that night and then continued walking right into his fucking trap like a dumb whore. You're supposed to be better than that!"

I wasn't going to let his words hurt me because this wasn't the Lev who'd played me music and walked me through my emotions just days ago. Lev was letting it all out, blaming me for his failed attempt to break free of his brother and the Solkov family but hating me and my lack of action. It wasn't my fault that Lev was born into this, nor was it mine that I was raised outside of it and dragged back into it.

"What exactly do you want from me, Lev?" I looked up into his eyes, and he looked confused. "Hm? Tell me exactly what to do in order to make this shitty situation any more bearable, and I'll do it. Point me in the direction of salvation, and I'll crawl on my hands and knees, but don't stand there and sneer down at me when you've bent your neck in submission your entire fucking life and have nothing to show for it."

I was very calm, but I could hear my blood rushing through my ears like a freight train with no destination. My hands shook, a damp sweat was on the back of my neck, and I was so tired. "Some days, I wish it would all just fade away," I told him as he remained silent. "I open my eyes in the morning and want to cry because I'm still here - I'm still me, and I know you feel the same way. So why are you making this hard on me?"

He breathed deeply, his shoulders rising and falling with every expanse of his lungs - shaking as if it hurt him to breathe. To be alive. Lev Solkov was a man of many threads, some ironed out and organised, like his love of art and music. Other pieces of him frayed from years of use, like his love affair with cocaine and blooding his knuckles by the command of his blood brother.

"I want you to be better than the world I regret dragging you into," Lev said. "*Milyy*, you are more than a place holder for my brother's business deals. You have the capacity to listen and care, even when it is not earned. I've watched you sit in that library for hours, smiling when the world would have sat crumbled and broken."

A stray tear fell from my eyes, and Lev's hand wiped it from my face. I was frozen for a moment, his warm hand on my cheek and the smell of Marlboro and Tom Ford wafting from him in waves that settled in my chest.

"I don't want blood on my hands, Lev. I can't be the reason that the Solkov bratva can destroy another family."

He nodded, "We have to get in contact with Alexei."

I pulled away from him, letting his hands drop between us. "Leo would kill you if he found out you went behind his back."

He scratched the back of his head, wincing a little. "I'm doing this for all of us. Leo doesn't need D.C; he just thinks he'll never be better than our father if he doesn't make something of his own."

I scoffed. "So he wants to be a better bratva boss than daddy dearest?

Follow in his footsteps by murdering an entire family?"

"It wouldn't be a massacre like with your family," Lev said, though I didn't believe him. "If Michael chooses not to leave, then Leo would have him killed but not his family."

"Oh," I exclaimed. "That makes it better because it's only going to be one life?"

"It means that Leo has no interest in wiping out a bloodline, unlike our father. Under all of the hatred you feel for him, can't you see that there is a chance he can be saved from turning into Vlad? Unlike you, Leo has never known anything outside of the bratva. From the day he was born, his destiny was written by our father and forced onto the masses like the second coming. He must be shown how to be Leo, the husband, instead of Vor Solkov."

I shook my head. "Why is it my responsibility to change a man who has no interest in changing for others?"

"Because you're the only one who can do it," Lev pleaded. "I've watched how Leo speaks to you and how he allows you to speak back to him. No one does that. And those bleeding crosses? It would have been far easier to let the families take their blood, but instead, he gave you the choice."

"An impossible choice!" I screamed while spinning in a circle in his room, feeling like I was going crazy. He couldn't actually believe that Leo could change, could he? "Leo needed my name more than he needed a dead Romanov."

Lev looked at me, and quietly, he said, "Leo could have let you die that night, but he didn't. What do you think my father would have done if he caught his own son committing treason just minutes after his ascent to the throne?"

My body was heated with anger. "Leo doesn't get a pass just because he did what was *right*. He shouldn't be rewarded for acting like a fucking human."

"You're right, but he did act like a human. That humanity is still in there, and you can bring it out."

I started walking back towards the door, reaching for the bottle that he'd sat on the counter. "I'm getting out of here," I muttered before Lev stepped in my way and knocked my hand aside.

"I'm not done here," he said while standing over me. "If you don't want to wake up every day with that deep pit of guilt - that roaring monster that follows you and stares at you from every corner of the room, then you have to get Alexei to take the seat."

I threw my hands into the air. "Why? What does it really matter to you?"

Lev stood there for a moment, his eyes pleading with me. "Because," he said slowly. "If you don't, and Leo takes D.C., I'll have lost my brother forever. There's no coming back from that."

Ana

I spent the rest of the night in my room without a bottle of vodka. Lev was correct; there was a chance I could avoid this and keep Leo in New York while also handing my brother his birthright back. The brotherhood of the seven owed Alexei a seat, and I needed to convince him that the only way to really avenge our family would be to prove that they failed. A Romanov still gained his throne.

I ventured down the stairs this morning, ready to spend another day locked in the library, when I spotted an older woman hunched over the stove. She heard me enter and turned to give me a tight nod but didn't speak. This must be Yulia, the cook Leo had told me was so great. As spiteful as I was that I never got to finish her pyrizhky, I was salivating at the mouth this morning.

"Sorry, I wasn't expecting anyone to be home."

She nodded and returned to her work, "Mr. Solkov told me you might make an appearance in my kitchen and that I'm to give you anything you need." Her eyes roamed over my body, and she shook her head, "Sit down; you could fall over with a gust of wind."

I wrinkled my nose at her attitude but decided not to argue with her - She was right, after all. Even after stuffing my face for a week, I was nowhere near where I should be for my height and age. The orphanage had instilled terrible eating habits in us girls, encouraging us only to eat when we became dizzy and that the pain meant progress.

I watched the woman continue her work for about twenty minutes, her hands moving expertly across the top of the pie crust to make intricate designs. "Can I ask you your name?" I interrupted the silence, her head snapping up to me like she had forgotten I was even there.

"You're the lady of the house, *da*? You can ask me anything you like," She answered before returning to work. I expected her to answer me, but then again, I guess she had.

She was a short woman, her hair completely silver and wrapped in a scarf that kept it out of her face as she worked. Her mouth had lines from laughter, and her eyes, though wrinkled, were still full of strength and life.

"My name is Ana," I offered her and was taken aback when she laughed.

"*Da*, everyone knows who you are. Never in my years did I think you'd be sitting in my kitchen, *nyet*, never in my years."

Of course, she knew who I was; it was likely most of New York did by now—the lost Bratva princess who was now hiding in the Solkov mansion. My fingers tapped across the table, itching for a cigarette. I hadn't smoked one in days, and I'd forgotten to bum one from Lev before he dashed out of the door this morning, close to Leo's heels, as they barely gave me a sideways glance. My husband hadn't tried to speak with me this morning, and I wondered if he'd heard any of Lev and I's conversation.

I hoped not.

The woman must have noticed my anxiety because she sighed loudly and dug into her apron. When she pulled out the red carton and threw it across the table at me, I'd never wanted to kiss an old woman so much.

As I was about to bring the filter to my lips, she hissed at me, "Outside! You and Levander the both - ruining the paint on these beautiful walls. I'm in her trying to cook a nice meal," she muttered before turning back around.

I winced, "Sorry."

Standing up, I walked towards the French doors in the dining room that I had looked out of on occasion, the snow piling on the back terrace and looking none too inviting, but I wasn't about to meet her wrath.

I stepped out into the cold and sighed, chasing away the crisp air with the burning smoke that brought life onto my lungs - and took it. I looked around the open space again and imagined how it could look come spring, the flower tressells overflowing, birds resting on the old brick walls. I could have a raised garden bed. Being out in the fresh air with my hands in the dirt had been one of life's little pleasures at the orphanage, and I hadn't been allowed to do it myself.

I was torn between wanting to make this place feel like a home and resenting it for what it was. A prison. It was a gilded cage for Leo Solkov to keep his pretty little prized jewel for all to see. I could either make my cage more inviting, or I could burn it to the ground. I threw my cigarette on the terrace and stomped the fire out before walking back into the warm house.

When I sat back down in the kitchen, I finally asked outright, "What is your name?" I already knew it, but I wanted her to tell me.

The old woman hummed and looked over her shoulder with a smile, "I'm Yulia, the cook. There are housekeepers as well, but they usually come once a week. Now that the newlyweds are," She paused and looked me over, "- anyways, they will likely start coming by again."

The sound of the front doorbell drew our attention to the hall. "I can get it," Yulia smiled tightly and walked towards the entrance hall. I padded after her and furrowed my brow as the bell continued to ring. "A moment! *Lisus*," She muttered before opening the door and looking straight down the barrel of a gun.

For a moment, everything was silent. I could see Yulia standing at the door, the masked gunmen hidden somewhere behind it, and then the sound came back as her body crumbled quickly to the ground.

The movies always make it seem like the body falls theatrically to the ground. Their knees bent, they cried out, then fell to the side. But that was far from the reality. Yulia's head ricocheted back, and she crumbled like a bag of lead bricks. I don't remember what the gunshot sounded like, but I think I'll remember the sound of her body hitting the ground for the rest of my life.

I was frozen in fear, my hands covering my mouth as the murderer stepped past the threshold, and two more came after them. They were all dressed in black, their faces masked with black bandannas while they looked around for what they came for. When they all looked at me, I knew.

I turned back into the kitchen and panicked, running down the side hall that I knew went to Leo's study. I tried opening the door, but it was locked. Shouting started from the kitchen, their voices loud and in Italian.

"Fuck," I muttered while trying all of the doors along the dark hall. When one finally clicked, I dashed inside and closed the door - popping the lock in place before turning around. I was standing in a conference room, a long table situated in the middle with many chairs around it. But there were windows, and we were still on the main level.

Looking out of the frost-coated glass, I could see the kitchen terrace off to my right, but right below me was a six foot drop. Though on the first floor, New York was known to have their basements with windows peaking just above street level. I would have to jump. A rattling at the door made me shake.

"Little *princespessa*! We know you're in there," A man sang from behind the wooden door.

I pushed the window open as the handle raddled. "Don't make this so difficult *bella*, we are here to help."

Yeah, fucking right.

Cold air filled the room, whipping my hair around and blowing the curtains around. I looked below me once more, knowing that I wouldn't be seriously hurt by the fall, but damn, a sprung ankle wouldn't be fun.

"Anastasia, come on out *bella*." They weren't pounding on the door, but I could hear them messing with the lock, so there was no time to waste. I said a quick prayer and jumped, the wind briefly blowing through my hair before I landed in the snow with a wince. My right ankle had a shooting pain.

Of course.

I took a step forward, the weight being manageable, before I ran across the back garden and tried the side gate. These townhouses had enclosed gardens with high walls, but they connected for safety. The iron gate swung open, and I dashed into the neighbour's area. I was barefoot with no jacket, limping through the yards and trying to decide how far I should go before trying to get into one of the other houses.

As I opened the third gate, I didn't hear footsteps behind me. All I could feel was the bite of the cold on my bare feet and the sharp pinch of a needle in my neck.

Leo

Four Hours Earlier

I stood before Ana's door, my hand clenched into a fist at my side as I told myself I wouldn't push her. But fuck, I wanted her bent across my knee and begging for forgiveness. I'd heard her run up the stairs and into Lev's room, and a less secure man would feel threatened by his bide running to his brother for support. I'd told myself in the beginning that I wasn't going to be able to be emotionally there for Ana.

It would be the job of the other Solkov brother.

Lev's outburst yesterday left me concerned for him because I know that Ana sees him as a friend while Lev sees her as a way out of his depression. She's a spotlight - a rope to hang onto and use to crawl out of his whole. I wasn't afraid of my brother stealing my wife; in fact, I didn't care if she received all of her emotional needs from him. I was worried about the day that Ana no longer needed him.

I heard him leave his room and turned to see him approaching me slowly from down the hall. He looked better this morning than yesterday. He had a fresh shave, and his eyes looked more alert and less sallow than usual. His gaze met mine, and he nodded towards her door.

"She'll be asleep for a while - I saw her light was on late, and she was probably reading."

I grunted. "Whatever you two are planning, I only ask that you consider the consequences of your actions." I turned away from the door and looked my brother in the eyes. "Neither of you are allowed to get yourselves in danger. You're assets to the Solkov Bratva."

Lev immediately sneered at me and moved to walk away, but I caught his arm and squeezed until I was sure he felt the pain. "I know you've been talking to her about the seat. I obviously can't control if Alexei takes it; I think you know that too, but consider the fallout if Alexei decides that Ana is important enough to him to set aside his grievances. She could be cannon fodder or worse."

His jaw was tight, and his eyes flickered to the closed door behind which Ana was nestled. "He won't hurt her." He tried to convince me.

I laughed, pulling him closer and whispering, "I would."

His eyes grew in alarm, and then anger.

"I wouldn't give up a throne for women I didn't know. If a girl came crawling out of the walls, swearing to be a love child of father and one of his whore's, I'd sooner put a bullet in her head than allow her to affect business."

Lev pushed his tongue into his cheek. "This isn't about business-."

"Oh, fuck off. It's always about business," I reminded him. "Now, Ana is my wife, and I would never allow someone to harm what's mine, but her feelings are of no consequence to me. I can live with a broken soul but not a broken body."

"You're a real piece of shit, you know that?"

I frowned, knowing the sort of monster I seemed like. I'd had a heart once, buried beneath pages of books and music just as Ana and Lev still did, but it had been cut out by my father and offered up in exchange for being the most powerful man on the East Coast. No, I wasn't going to go out of my way to hurt Ana or make her feel hopeless, but at the end of the day, she would be alive, and that's what mattered.

That's what I promised myself I would do all those years ago. Keep her alive.

"Just do your fucking job and get to the docks. I have two shipments coming in this afternoon, and the yard hands need to be filled with money before they'll let us unload."

I thought he was going to argue with me for a moment, but then he dutifully nodded and walked back down the hall. I turned one more time to stare at the closed door, wishing with everything inside of me that our lives could be different, but knowing that this was the destiny we were born into.

* * *

I arrived at the office earlier than usual that morning in preparation for a meeting with the brotherhood. We met once a month outside of notable events in order to air grievances or simply get drunk away from prying eyes. Many of the men here rarely ate or consumed alcohol outside of their own homes, the paranoia driving most of the brotherhood to be recluses. After my father exhibited an ability to get rid of those even as powerful as the Romanovs, no one felt safe.

I stared at the wedding band on my finger, gold and cold staring right back at me.

I had a wife.

One who fought me hated me and hissed in my direction every chance she got, but she was beautiful while she did it. I would hate the day she ever stopped fighting me - she lost her spirit. It's why I hated myself most days. I knew that everything I've been working towards in D.C. could be the end of a future with Ana, but not taking it back meant that Alexei would have the opportunity to get closer to my family.

I don't care what Lev says; Alexei was dangerous. I was not willing to bet my entire life on the whims of an emotionally stunted young man with a pension for removing heads. I strongly doubted that Ana would be enough to turn him in because I knew that it wouldn't stop me. If someone took my family like that, nothing would slow me down.

I sat back in my office that overlooked an endless building skyline and cursed when a knock at the door ruined my peace. "*Chto?*"

Lev walked into my office with Antonio Barone behind him, looking pale. He was the eldest son of the Barone mafia, and we often worked together to settle shipment territories and even deal among us. His old man had been a piece of work and didn't believe in doing business with anyone outside of the Italians.

I quirked a brow at Lev, who shrugged and sat in the back of the room. "What can I do for you, Antonio?" The man had never looked this rattled, with his black hair pushed straight back and sweat pooling at his brow. He glanced behind him at Lev and cleared his throat. "I need to speak with you. Privately."

Every nerve in my body went on edge as I stared him down. Antonio and I had kept a good working relationship for years, but no one was truly loyal. Everyone had a price - a greater motivation than peace. I motioned for Lev to leave, but knew he'd be right outside the door.

"Sit down, Antonio. You're making me nervous." We both took a seat, myself behind the desk and Antonio falling uneasily into the leather chair across from me.

"First, I want to tell you that I came straight here after hearing about it. I told you I wouldn't go against the family, but what my father is doing could tear us all apart, and I want *nothing* to do with it."

I leaned across the wide table and growled. "What. Happened."

He took a deep breath. "My father has decided to move against you, and he's taking out the docks tonight."

"Fucking Christ," I cursed. "He's going to do all this while the brotherhood tries to prevent war with Alexei?"

The usually calm man vibrated in his seat, eyes watching my hands. The greatest weapons in the room. "He wants to run the brotherhood out of New York for good, which means cutting the head off the snake."

"He's going to try and assassinate me?"

"No."

"Then what? He knows I won't leave this city alive." He likely teamed up with the Bianchis to make a move on all of New York - a place once run by the Italians. They'd been trying to reclaim it for decades, but their old ways kept them out of drugs and stuck in the past. The average age of a Don was fifty, while the vors were all under thirty-five. I'd always hoped Antonio would take his father's seat, but I also questioned what that power would do to a reliable ally.

Antonio leaned forward and placed his hands on the oak desk. "Remember Leo, I came straight here. I -".

"Out with it, Barone."

"He knows your pockets run too deep, so he needs to drain them. He's going to blackmail you for everything you have, Leo."

I sneered. "He has nothing on me. All of my sins have been committed in the daylight."

"Everyone knows that it's why he took Ana."

I lurched from my seat and rounded the desk instantly, grabbing Antonio's shirt and pulling him to his feet. "If they touch a hair on her head, I'll burn Little Italy to the ground with all of you guineas inside of it. One big grease fire," I growled in his face. Lev burst through the door at the same time, his eyes alight and a gun in his hands.

Antonio stuttered, "They're moving - they're moving soon. She'll be out of Brooklyn by now."

I flickered my gaze to my brother, but he was already out of the door, likely in a mad dash back to the house to see if she was still there. But I knew that if Antonio was here, then she was already gone.

"What does your father think he will get out of me but threatening my wife? Hm?" My fingers wrapped around Antonio's neck, his face turning red as I squeezed. "A wife for a son? No, a wife is far more valuable in our world. She can produce unlimited heirs. A Romanov wife? I wonder how many heads I'll be able to collect," I said with a feline smile.

"Please, Leo, I came straight to you. I don't want a war," tears started to swell in the young man's eyes. "I have a wife and kid, too, Leo. This isn't what I want."

I looked down my nose at him. "Maybe so, but I'll need the location of all the Barone safe houses."

He winced. "I can't do that."

Before he could even react, my right fist flew up and smashed into his Roman nose, and I watched it explode in blood. "Fuck!" He shouted as his head lolled to the side.

I grabbed him around the collar again, swinging him around until his back was against my desk. "Let's try this again. Where are the Barone and Bianchi safe houses?"

He was panting, his legs losing footing below him. "I have family in those safe houses, Leo!" He shouted at me while tears started to fall from his eyes. "If I give you the locations, you'll take out everyone in them, and most of the family is innocent."

He was right, of course; I would rather burn down the entire block than worry about friendly fire right now. But I wasn't letting him out of here without those locations. There must have been a dozen safe houses across the city and onto the island - impossible for my men to search all at once.

"If you don't give me the locations, I'll just get to your home, Antonio." He choked on a plea, his chest shaking as I shook my head. "I'll go to your daughter's school and your wife's church, and you'll be another name wiped from the map, just like the Romanovs." The threat tasted bitter on my tongue, and I would never hurt his little girl, but he didn't know that. Everyone knew the story of what my father did, and it made the Solkovs look wild. Unpredictable.

"No!" He shouted as his hands clawed at my own. "Fuck! Leo, please, man. I want to help!"

"THEN HELP ME FIND MY WIFE!"

Antonio was understandably reluctant to give me the information, so I had to become persuasive.

I wiped my hands and threw the bloodied rag onto the floor beside the eldest Barone heir. I hadn't planned on getting my hands dirty today, but when he refused to give up the safe house in fear of his family, I had to convince him it was in his best interest. I knew he would have held out for too long if I hadn't taken out my knife. I dropped the tip of his ring finger beside him. Antonio coughed onto the floor, staining my favourite rug, before turning on his back.

"Don't hurt my mother. Leo, please."

I stepped over him and opened the side panel of my closet before pulling my jacket over my shoulders. Lev left when Antonio said her name, but it was too late. Ana was taken from our home, and a bullet was put in Yulia's head.

"I appreciate your warning, Antonio, but the sins of the father, *unfortunately*, stain the son. You'll leave New York tonight with your sister - I don't care where, but the Barones are no longer welcome in New York."

Ana was being held at Antonio's family home, a place that had been in his family for generations near Lake Peekskill. Not far from St. Basil's. I would burn it to the ground along with anyone who helped. I opened the door to leave but stopped, remembering a bloodied family crumbled on the floor of their basement with gunshots littering their best dresses and tuxedos. "Go to New Orleans with your wife and daughter, and don't come back. I'll do my best for your mother."

I closed the door behind me and hoped I'd never see his face again because I hated feeling regret.

Ana

I could hear people talking around me, but their voices were hushed and far away. I could tell I was lying down with my head on a pillow, the fabric brushing my cheeks, and my hair splayed across my face like a curtain.

"It'll take a few days to know, but look at her."

"I want all eyes on the Barones and their soldiers. I don't trust the fucking wops not just to take everything and run. Elio would sell his own children for a decent seat at the table." His voice was deep and lacking any discernible accent.

"The Bianchis guaranteed their corporation -". Another low voice said, but he was interrupted.

"They're all the same! Just watch them, okay? I'm not losing everything to the fucking Italians."

I took a breath, but when I tried to exhale, it turned into a cough that racked my entire body. My shoulders shook as I opened my eyes and took a groggy look around me, the room being all dark wood and smelling of cigars.

"*Zdravstvuy,*" a man said, drawing my attention to the two suit-clad men peering at me front behind a desk. Fuck, I was sure it was Italians who took me, so if they were working with a sect of Russians . . .

I pushed myself the rest of the way up and blinked; the taller of the two men walked around the desk and stopped a healthy distance from me with his hands tucked in his pants and a guarded look on his handsome face. He was pale and had blonde hair shaved down short and bright blue eyes squinting at me. I'd never seen him around the house, but Leo had hundreds of men across the city.

"Do you not speak Russian?" He asked me while I continued to stare at him. *"Ona bespolezna,"* he muttered over his shoulder to the other asshole who was still staring at me. His partner was a large man, big around the gut but short in stature, with a stereotypical leather jacket, stretched tight over his shoulders. When I leaned forward and spat onto the posh carpet below us, I watched his fists clench at his side.

"If I'm useless, then why am I here?"

The blond one's eyes widened before he smirked. "So she does speak."

"And spits." His partner said with malice.

I flipped him off with a smile before looking back at the other one. "What am I doing here?" My head still felt heavy from whatever drug they'd hit me with, and my throat was dry as the desert.

The man walked closer to me, dark tattoos lining his neck as he got down on one knee next to the leather couch I'd been lying on. "Can you tell me your name?"

"Ana," I responded immediately, and he hummed while shaking his head. "No, can you tell me your *family* name?"

I held up my hand with my wedding band and grinned. "Solkov."

His eyes flashed to the side as his jaw tightened. "Do you know who I am, *krasnyy?*"

I crossed my arms, sitting back against the couch and closing my mouth. I had to be careful with what information I gave them because Leo would be here soon. I had to hold out until he came for me. He would come for me, right?

He rubbed his hand over his face while the other dickhead continued to complain from his side of the room. "She knows nothing," he kept muttering.

"Will you shut up?!" Blondie shouted at him, and it was silent once more. I grinned, knowing who the boss was. "There are only two outcomes to this, so if you want out of this room alive, I need you to answer some questions for me. Do you *know* who your family is?"

I laughed. "I thought everyone already knew my story. The concussed *bratva printsessa* who was found by the King of New York."

He sneered. "That usurper cock-sucker couldn't find a rat in New York, let alone stumble upon Anastasia Romanov. What did he offer you in exchange for your part in all of this?" His eyes scanned over me again, my gaze studying the carpet pattern. "Money? Power?"

I didn't answer him. It sounded like he was trying to imply that I wasn't really Ana, and if that was the case, then I was in severe danger. If they thought I was pulled from the streets, which I was, but if they thought I was lying, then there wasn't a family name to protect me. They'd already attacked the Solkov home, so what more could they do?

"You're Russian; we were able to confirm that, at least from the orphanage. Is that why you show loyalty to a man who, I hear, treats you more like a prisoner than a bride? You think that he's going to protect you?"

I met his gaze this time, our blue eyes locked on one another. "Such is marriage for a woman like me. We're all prisoners to its rules and expectations within the bratva."

"No." He shook his head, "Such is marriage to a bastard like Leo. You must have been so young when his father butchered the Romanovs - too young to understand that his hands are stained far beyond the sins of his father."

"Who are you?"

He smiled. "I'm the root that was forgotten about - allowed to take hold and grow stronger than ever imagined."

My blood went cold, my heart pumping as his grin grew broader and more sinister. "I'm the man who's sister you're impersonating."

I opened my mouth but quickly closed it. "Alexei?" I looked at him this time; his high cheekbones and bright blue eyes that many told me were a trademark of the Romanovs. The little boy from the pictures and brother that I couldn't remember.

He nodded. "I have to admit that Leo did a great job at casting a grown Ana; your hair is just as red as I remember hers being." His fingers reached out and wrapped around one of my stray strands. "But Ana is dead, and the tests will confirm Leo's treachery once more."

"What tests?" If he were talking about a DNA test, it would prove who I was.

Alexei looked over his shoulder to the man who was still silent. "What is worse, Mikey?" Alexei smiled, "Is it to stand by while your betrothed is butchered or drag a poor little orphan into our world and parade her around as the long-lost little sister?"

I shook my head, "Leo was only a boy when his father rebelled. He's only trying to -."

"Avoid a war?" Alexei said before I could. "Yes, I think we've all heard the same line a few too many times by now. The great and noble King of New York wishes to prevent bloodshed. Meanwhile, he butchers Italians from the East River to the Lower Bay and plans an assault on D.C."

I clenched my teeth. "He can't touch D.C. if you take your seat on the council."

Alexei's hand shot out and wrapped around my face, his thumb digging into the side of my cheek until it *hurt*. "No, *krasnyy*, because my birthright is New York. I've been hiding among the Italians in the windy city for too long, and I'm ready to show the world that a Romanov will always have a divine right to the Big Apple. A city that abandoned a man who gave his life to the community saw the church through the second fall of the Motherland and promised me a future of adoration." Alexei released me roughly before stepping away. "And I will either be adored or feared here."

I frowned, picturing a tiny little boy covered in his family's blood. He was so young when everything happened, but if he was raised with those memories and a hatred for the Solkovs, I wondered if I could erase all that.

"Alexei, it's really me. It's Ana -."

"How do you know? Hm? Is it because they told you so and promised you a life of comfort? Is it worth the bullet that I could easily put through your skull?"

I shook my head, tears brimming in my eyes as I stared into his gaze, which was just as blue as mine. "I remember her laugh and the golden locket around her neck."

Shock flitted across Alexei's face momentarily before it was wiped away. "Pretty pictures of a mother who's nothing but bones now. Did Leo also tell you stories about my sister, Olga? She was beautiful, too, but no one could hold a candle to Maria. Her blonde hair reached down her back, always braided by our mother. Or Tatiana? She was the spitting image of our father, with *none* of his cruelty. They were innocent!"

I shook my head, crying. "I can't remember them," I admitted. "Sometimes I wish I could, but I can see now that it was a blessing that it was taken from me. I can't image the pain you must feel, Alexei, living every day with the ghosts of them."

His lips curled back over his teeth, and his hands tightened my throat. "They would still be here if it wasn't for the Solkovs. Can't you see that? Their ghosts will always haunt me until Leonid and Levandr are long forgotten in the dirt."

My vision was going fuzzy, the lack of oxygen making my head feel light. "I'm still here, Alexei. I'm so sorry I wasn't able to go with you."

The young man's eyes studied me closely, roaming over my hair and across my cheeks. "The test will come back soon, and when it proves that you're a liar, I'll cut your beautiful blue eyes from your head for daring to even look like her. To look like Anastasia," he whispered.

I flinched back, fear and anger pooling in my gut. "You're psychotic."

He smiled. "I'm willing to be, *printessa*."

Suddenly, his head whipped around as shouting came from behind the large oak door. "You don't think . . ." The other man muttered as Alexei stormed towards the commotion. As his hand wrapped around the brass handle, a gunshot sounded from somewhere in the building.

Leo.

Alexei looked towards me and frowned. "He's a fool to think I'd let you leave here alive."

I forced myself to smile through the anxiety and fear that was running in my veins. "And if it's true? Would you kill your sister, Alexei?"

I could see the rage behind his eyes - the doubt. He could see our mother in my face, even if I couldn't remember her. He was a man who was ready to burn all of New York down for his family, and he knew one of them might have been still alive. Staring at him with red welts around her neck, pleading for him to reconsider.

He closed his eyes before charging me, his face inches from mine as more gunshots rang out. "You stay right fucking here, or I'll kill you myself. *Ponyal?*"

I swallowed. *"Ponyal."*

He stared down for a few more seconds before he swore, turning back towards the door with his grunt and disappearing into the growing chaos.

The moment the door shut behind them, I flew from my seat and yanked on the handle to find it locked from the outside. "Fuck."

I looked around the large office, thinking that a crime syndicate *had* to store weapons in every room. I found two pistols in the library two days ago but had no courage to pick them up. Even after living years on the streets, I'd avoided touching them at all costs. Some of my friends would bring them out, smiling wickedly and laughing, but I never had to stomach for it.

My hands rummaged over the bookshelves, feeling around the back of drawers as more and more screams filled the hallways. The shots were getting louder and closer.

A terrifying thought popped into my head - what if this wasn't Leo? What if it was someone who also wanted the Romanov princess under their thumb and knew the right place to steal her from? After all, Alexei had done the heavy lifting getting me out of the townhouse.

As the screams grew, I wrapped my fingers around a heavy statue that sat atop the dark shelving. My hands shook - either from fear or the drug that still ran through my veins. I ran to the opposite side of the desk, ducking to scramble below it as the oak door blew to pieces. I covered my mouth with my hand, trying to suppress the scream that built into my lungs.

I heard the heavy footsteps over debre and more gunshots from further away, but the most significant threat was in the room. His steps were slow - deliberate even as he came closer to the desk that was my cover. By the way, he kicked in that door, I knew I would be no match for him, the heavy statue feeling even more leaden in my hands.

As a pair of black shoes stopped before me, I held my breath. We both stayed there - not moving for a moment in complete silence. My body was rigged as I imagined the things they'd do to me. When his toes lifted to walk away, I thought I'd done it.

I was safe.

But then a hand reached under the table, latched onto the collar of my sweater, and dragged me out from under the table. I screamed, swinging my arms wildly as I held onto the heavy figurine until I felt it make contact with something solid. My attacker shouted, releasing me as I dropped my weapon and stumbled around the desk. I ran over the broken door and was almost around the corner when a set of arms wrapped around my shoulders and yanked me back.

"No! No, fuck you!" I screamed as the man shook me back and forth.

"Ana!"

"Let me go, you fucking cock sucker! You -".

"*Milyy!*"

I froze, my chest heaving as tears stained my cheeks. The man whipped me around, so I was staring right into his brown eyes, and I wanted to cry. "Lev?"

His hands came up around my shoulders as he nodded. "It's me, it's just me. You're okay."

A sob caught in my throat at the sight of the familiar face. His eyes were bloodshot, as usual, but they were safe. I wanted to collapse, but more shouting came down the dimly lit hall. "Where's Leo?" My eyes searched over his shoulders, but Lev quickly took my hand and started pulling me down the hall.

"Buying us time."

We started to run down the halls, and I quickly realised we weren't in some building - it was a home. The walls were lined with old family photos, and houseplants lined the large windows—a magnificent house filled with screams and gunfire.

As we came to another corner, Lev stopped, turning around and pushing me flat against the wall so that his body covered mine. His dark eyes looked down at me in warning. More footsteps sounded from close by, loud voices shouting orders in Italian. Lev grabbed me and started to back us down the hall we'd just come from - but more voices filled the space.

"Shit," Lev muttered as we dashed into an empty guestroom. As the door closed, the hall we'd just escaped from was peppered with gunshots. Lev pushed me back further into the dark room while men exchanged bullets and profanity just on the other side of the door.

"How are we going to get out of here?"

Lev looked at me from the corner of his eye before pulling a pistol from his waistband and checking the magazine. "We wait for Le. He gave me strict orders to get you out safely, and I can't do that when the hallways are a war zone."

"He's not out there alone, is he?" I asked furiously.

Lev nodded. "An informant came to us after you were taken, and Leo got your location out of him. There were trucks of men on their way, but he wouldn't wait for them. You should have seen the look in his eyes when Antonio said you were gone."

It makes sense because there was nothing valuable about a dead Romanov—no heirs to be had when I was in the dirt.

"Just do as I say, and hopefully, we can all get out of here in one piece - those fucking Italians are viscous," Lev swore.

"It's not just the Italians, Lev. It's Alexei."

His head whipped up. "What did you fucking say?"

I shook my head. "It was Alexei who took me, with help from the Italians. He said something about Bianchis. He drugged me, and I woke up in that office before all hell broke loose. Lev, he doesn't believe that I'm Ana."

"*Yebat'*," he swore as he slammed his fist into the wall. "You couldn't have mentioned that before now?!"

"I'm sorry, I was too busy thinking about if someone was coming to *kill* me and the constant volley of gunshots!" We continued to shout at one another as the shots grew closer.

He threw his hands in the air, "What did you say to him?"

I crossed my arms and bit my tongue. I'd set his piano on fire if we made it out of this alive.

"You're not listening! He doesn't want a seat from Chicago, Lev. He wants New York and won't let me get in the way of him taking the throne back."

The door burst open in a cloud of smoke and wood chippings as Lev turned to put the barrel of his gun in the face of the intruder. I leapt behind the bed right as I heard Lev hit the ground with a grunt, and the relieving sound of Leo's voice filled the room.

"I could hear you two squabbling like children from down the fucking hall! Get up!" He growled at Lev, but when his eyes met mine as I stood from where I'd been kneeling, I could see the relief on his beautiful features. His white button-up was sprayed with blood, and his face was covered in sweat and soot while his eyes roamed over me.

"I'm okay." I forced a smile onto my face as he marched towards me. "Leo, I'm oka -".

His lips smashed into mine as his arms created a cage around my body. He tasted like salt and whiskey and sweet, sweet relief. Too soon, he pulled away and ran his hands over my face. *"Lischka."* His firm fingers settled around the nape of my neck, warm and strong. I'd be lying if I said I didn't melt into his touch.

"It was Alexei," I whispered to him. "He's here."

Leo

She was in my arms. She was okay. But Alexie was here, which meant that only one of us was making it out of here alive. He'd gone so far as to take Ana from our home; there would be little I could say to him as a shield against his wrath.

Her beautiful red hair was curling around her shoulders, hiding a faint bruise that was forming on her neck. My eyes lingered on the marks, wanting to cut off the hands of whoever did this to her.

"He doesn't believe I'm Ana and wants that seat. He wants it, but not from Chicago." She was panting, eyes wide as I held her close to me. "Please, Leo, he doesn't understand that you didn't have a part in the murders. He wants to kill both of you." She looked over her shoulder at Lev, who watched her with the intensity of a wolfhound. His eyes were blown out, his arms jittery at his sides.

I grabbed her shoulders and pulled her back, staring down into her watery eyes. It must have been a lot for her to see him for the first time and have it be like this. "If he sees the test come back, he might still wage the war he came here for. I'm sorry, Ana, but Alexei will never stop trying to kill me."

She shook her head. "You have to give him a chance. Please," She begged as her hands clung to my biceps. "He's all I have left."

I tried not to let the hurt show on my face because I knew that it was my fault she felt this way. I could have been nicer and more understanding of what she's gone through. My father might have been cruel, but I'd never known what it was like to sleep on a park bench and wonder where my next meal would come from. I'd never been alone because Lev and I had each other, even when we were too broken to do anything but drink and kill.

I looked over at my brother and the destruction on his face that had been caused by years of abuse from our father that just spilled over into my years as vor. I sighed, "I'll give him one chance. If he gives up his seat, I'll let him live."

Ana's face screwed up in anger before she quickly bottled it, moving out of my grasp and closer to Lev. Her arms wrapped around herself as she glanced down at the floor. "Fine."

I looked to Lev, who grunted, meaning it was better not to push it right now. I knew this would not end this conversation, but there was no time to argue. I moved forward and gently pushed Ana back into my brother's arms, moving them out of the way before I opened the door back into the war zone.

Smoke filled the hallways, but otherwise, it was mostly silent. I could hear shouting from outside and knew that my men had likely drawn their attention out of the house. "Stay with Lev, no matter what. Okay?"

Ana frowned but gave me a short nod before we stepped out of the room's safety. My hands were raised, finger on the trigger as he inched our way through the dark house that was littered with bullet holes and bodies. I could hear Lev whispering to Ana from behind, *"Keep your eyes on the back of his head. Don't look down."*

I stepped around a corner and shot back as a bullet grazed my cheek and exploded into the wall down the hall. I winced, pulling my head away but knowing that I'd been hit. Warm blood started to pool down my face, and Ana's hands wrapped around my arms to try and pull me back.

"L'ho preso!" One of the bastards shouted from his hiding place. They

were stationed towards the end of the hall, and I knew that if I didn't fire back then, they would start approaching sooner.

"Leo!" Ana gasped as I raised my hand and saw that my sleeve was already soaking through. The cut was superficial, but head wounds bled like a fucker.

"Take her down the back," I grit out to my brother, who was already pulling my wife from me. "Once you're off the property, call Igor and only him." Several safe houses had been set up in case something like this happened, and the only one I'd told Lev to take Ana to was further south than any of the Italians could find.

"No," Ana's hands caught onto my shirt again and tried to pull me back. "You're coming with us!"

I ignored her, knowing I might break if I stared into her eyes. But I couldn't risk them following us. I looked to my brother, "You keep her safe. If she dies, you die."

His face was stern, clutching Ana to his chest as she fought him. *"Da, brat."*

"No!" She tried to shout before Lev's hand clasped over her mouth, and she started dragging her back down the hall as she fought him. I watched my brother pull my wife away from me, her eyes blown wide in panic as she flayed and squirmed, but I knew she would never get out of his hold. Lev would keep her alive no matter what, even if that meant leaving me here.

As they were about to disappear down the opposite hall, I gave them a tight smile and said something I never thought I'd ever mean.

"Ya tebya lyublyu."

I love you.

She stopped struggling, her face going slack with shock before Lev pulled her around the corner and out of sight.

I told myself she would be okay, but this was the only way to ensure she escaped. The truth was, I feared meeting Alexei again because I didn't know how I'd feel once I looked into his eyes again. I hadn't seen him since I pulled Ana off of him in the basement of their family home.

I told myself for years that what happened to that family was because of my father, but what would I think when I was in the same room as him? Knowing that I had blackmailed his sister into marrying me - though it was she who bewitched me and now holds me captive on her island.

I reached into my pocket and pulled out a clip, seeing that it was half empty. I had six bullets between me and the Barone mafia. I took a deep breath, reloading my gun and saying a small prayer to a god I knew would never welcome me to his kingdom.

Ana

He loved me.

Lev's hold was like iron, dragging me backwards through the wild maze of hallways and rooms until we came out of the lower level and onto a patio backed into a line of trees. It dawned on me that we weren't anywhere near Brooklyn anymore and likely further north. The extensive grounds were covered in snow, knee high, staring back at us as if to say, *'I dare you.'*

I continued to kick, fighting Lev as he dragged me out of the house and into the dark forest that surrounded the manor. The snow stuck to my feet, seeping through my leggings and cloth trainers. I wanted to cry as a volley of gunshots could be heard from inside, wishing that he'd put aside his fucking ego and left with us.

Lev suddenly stopped and cussed under his breath. "Our men aren't here yet."

What? Lev and Leo had come here alone?

Lev removed his hand from around my mouth and spun me so I was looking at him. "We need to get away from here, Ana. I need you to run because I can't carry you through the snow. Whoever pulled in is not Solkov, so we must get you out of here."

"You can't just leave him there," I begged him. I grasped Lev's sleeves and tried pulling him back towards the grey, ornate manor that loomed over us. "He'll die in there!"

"I was given an order," he hissed. "Keep. You. Alive. I can't do that from inside of that fucking house." His hands grabbed me and started pulling me through the trees, the sun setting over the horizon and casting us into shadows. The sky was a deep pink, and the clouds looked heavy.

But he loved me.

He wouldn't tell me that and allow himself to die, would he? He wouldn't be so cruel?

"I know what's going through your head, but I need you to keep moving for me. Okay *milyy*?"

I swallowed down the pain in my chest, forcing my legs to move as he yanked me through the path that led to uncertainty. "They're going to kill each other," I said through a lump in my throat. My brother and my husband were in there, and only one would walk out alive.

And he loved me.

That was the worst part of all this because no one had ever said that to me before, and I wasn't sure how I felt in response. My husband says he loved me as I'm dragged away, knowing I may never see him again.

I hated him, and fuck, I might love him too.

Lev held onto my hand as we dashed through the dark forest, my face freezing in place and my feet numb from the wet cold that seeped through. Lev's hand was warm in mine, but it held me so tight I thought I might never have feeling in it again.

We tried to keep up our pace, but a half-drugged alcoholic and a cocaine addict could only get so far in knee-deep snow before both of us thought we'd collapse.

"Fuck," Lev said through giant gasps. "Without the sun, I have no idea where we are. We should have reached the road by now."

The forest was dense, so the snow wasn't as high under the thick canopy, but it was also so dark that it was hard to see Lev as he stood right in front of me. I turned in a circle, looking around until I saw a break in the treeline. "Over there," I pointed towards the clearing.

Lev and I started walking towards it, his hand in mine still as we tried to stay quiet and low to the ground. God, I was so cold. Both of us shook from the freezing air and adrenaline that was starting to wear off. The treeline opened up to a small field blanketed in white and lit with a soft grey glow as the clouds kept most of the moon's light hidden. The area surrounding the field was fenced in with tall pines, like the ones we just walked out of.

There had to be something nearby. We weren't far enough out of New York to be this barren. "Lev, where was the manor located?"

His eyes were carefully roaming the treeline, his spare hand clasping his pistol that weighed heavy on us both. "It's on Lake Peekskill, about an hour and a half from home."

"Peekskill," I said to myself. That was north of the city, just east of the Hudson. I guessed that we'd been walking for nearly three hours in the dark, and fuck if I didn't wish we could see the sky. I took another step into the clearing, squinting around to see if there were any property markers.

"I'm not familiar with this part of New York."

I didn't turn to look at him, but I did respond. "We might be close to the Hudson Highland State Park ." If we were, that meant we were close to St. Basil's. "What day is it?"

Lev thought about it for a moment before answering. "I think - I think it's the twenty-third." The night before Christmas Eve and the Nutcracker concert the orphanage always puts on yearly. Forcing parent-less children to dress up and perform in a near-empty auditorium—all empty except for the bishop and a few close benefactors.

"We can't go back the way we came," I said to him as he agreed. "If we're lucky, we'll hit the Albany Post Road and can take it to the orphanage."

Lev shook his head immediately. "I'm supposed to call. Ignore the moment we're safe."

"Yeah," I said as I spun around and growled. "And what classifies as safe these days? We have three options; only one has warm blankets that wouldn't be wrapped around us like body bags. The bratva funds St. Basil's, right?"

Lev looked weary but nodded. "Leo still writes checks every month."

"So they should have no problem opening their chapel to Christians in need, hm? *Russian Christians*," I emphasised. Though the church would like not to admit it, there was a difference between the Orthodox and Catholics. If the Italians came knocking, the church would be far kinder to their patrons than those who followed the Vatican.

Lev thought about it for a moment before he agreed. "Fine, but we're calling Igor the moment we are there. We'll rest until he picks us up."

Right, because that should give me enough time to get a message to Alexei, and I knew exactly who could do it.

Lev and I continued through the forest for another hour; our pace slowed significantly due to our freezing clothes and the snow that clung to our bodies. Finally, I heard the sound of a car passing. We edged to the end of the forest, where a two-lane road sat heavily salted and mostly barren of cars. There wasn't a lot out here, and the winters were so terrible that many avoided this part of Garrison, New York, until summer.

I looked ahead at a road sign and felt relief to see Bear Mountain Beacon Highway outlined in the distance. We were close. Lev and I crossed over the road, running into the other sense path of trees and keeping to the forest as we walked north towards the orphanage. Before long, I saw the familiar iron fence rusted through and the giant rock wall that announced the entrance to Saint Basil's. Of course, they now call it an *Academy*—a place for troubled youth.

'We Bring the Light of Christ to Young Lives', the sign declared to all

who passed their gates.

I felt my body heat with anxiety because I'd promised myself a long time ago that I'd never return here, most definitely not in need of help. But this wasn't just about me, and I could see Lev's lips turning blue, though he'd never complain. No, I was doing this because there was a man there that I knew could give me answers. He never missed the Christmas concert, and I was betting Leo's life on that now.

The gates were open, lightly decorated with garland with two huge signs that read, NO TRESPASSING. AREA UNDER SURVEILLANCE.

But as a teen, I quickly discovered that those signs were meant to scare me and that the cameras were not plugged into anything but overgrown bushes and crumbling rock walls.

We started the walk up St Basil's Road, past the Archbishop's house, until we saw the monstrous stone building rise from the snow. The building looked straight from an X-Men movie, and you might even think Professor X was hiding behind those stained glass windows.

But he wasn't, and no one was saving the world from their stone prison funded by dirty money and blood.

Lev held onto me, constantly tugging me back when the light would catch us. I finally spun around and hissed, "They can't help us if we don't ask!"

He looked torn between throwing me over his shoulder and allowing me to drag him to the side entrance. The kitchen doors were often left unlocked, drawing less attention than coming through the front.

We rounded the back, and a soft glow came from the windows and the faint smell of gingerbread. It was a treat the nuns would allow us after the concerts and considered a great *gift* from the church.

I let my hand rest on the stained door, remembering many nights of pushing through the kitchens and trying to disappear into the woods. Now, I was coming back with my own bratva in tow. Lev leaned in, "Are you sure about this?"

I gave him a quick nod. "They're the only ones who wouldn't turn us into the Italians. A service to the church binds them, and by extension, that includes its orphans and benefactors."

Many of the children graduated at eighteen and went straight to work with the Solkov Bratva, or made connections to other families along the east coast. It was a blessing and curse to be a man in this world because though the women appeared to be under the control of our male counterparts, it was the men who signed their names in blood and dedicated their lives to organised crime. The young boys were taught how to fight, while the girls were made to dance and look ethereal on the stages.

I pushed open the door, wincing at the long creak before feeling the oven's heat hit me like a brick. The lights were dim here, the floor of a grey stucco that kept it warm all winter. I pulled Lev in after me, shaking the snow from our clothes before we closed the door and sagged against it with relief.

"Anazelina?"

I looked up as a nun walked into the kitchen, her hands carrying a large pot of dough. Sister Ionna was tall and whispy-looking, a woman under her habit and thick dress. Her grey eyes were wrinkled at the corners from years of squinting at the stage, and her hands were thin and bony.

"Sister," I said before taking a careful step towards her. Sister Ionna's eyes glanced from Lev to me, taking in our wet attire and blue faces. "I need help."

Her face was unreadable, a symptom of orthodoxy, and she carefully set the pot down on the counter. "We were joyed to hear about your nuptials to Mr. Solkov," she said carefully. "The church has long maintained a close relationship with his family, and the children greatly benefit from his patronage."

She thought I had run away from him—a scared girl, running from her bratva husband.

"My husband will be elated to hear that his hard-earned money is making a great difference here," I said carefully, looking over my shoulder at Lev. "My brother-in-law here tells me that Leo would like to increase his donations to the home, but we need warmer clothes before we can discuss numbers."

Her brow quirked, looking over my sopping clothes and now wet floor. "Mr. Solkov knows that you are here?"

I swallowed past the lump in my throat. "My husband is in the middle of - of." I stuttered before continuing. "Difficult business negotiations."

"With the Barone's," Lev chimed in from behind.

I nodded. "We just came from their beautiful family home. Took a nice stroll through the forest even."

Sister Ionna's eyes fell, and she slowly understood. "And did the Barones know where you would be heading after you left?"

I shook my head. "We had to make a sudden departure, but I know many would look down their nose at such a home. They take communion elsewhere," I said firmly. A reminder that we were one.

Her high cheekbones cut into her thin face, and she looked as if she could deny us. Throw us out and tell us we knew better than to bring trouble to her door. "Head to my office," she finally said quietly. "I will bring you something dry."

She turned around and left, and I finally breathed before spinning around to see Lev shaking near the door. His lips were quivering, and his nose was a bright red. "Follow me," I said as I took his hand and led him through the back halls towards Sister Ionna's office, where I'd spent many hours as a girl. I could hear the sound of leather hitting skin in my head, but I shoved those memories aside.

Once tucked into the small office, housing but one desk and two backless stools, I let Lev collapse onto the ground. "I thought she was going to send us off," he muttered as I grabbed his hands and brought them to my lips. I was trying to breathe a little life back into them, though my own were numb.

"You don't need to do that, Ana." He said while trying to pull away, but I stabbed him with a stern look.

"I'm used to cold fingers and toes. I almost lost a foot two winters ago when shelters were overflowing, and I was lucky enough to tuck into the back of a liquor store because the man felt too guilty to leave me on the sidewalk." I smiled, thinking of that man. "He gave me a small nip of Vodka and his lunch. His name was Ajay, and he still offers up his store room for emergencies."

I looked up when Lev didn't say anything and saw the sympathy in his eyes that made me want to vomit. I never wanted sympathy, let alone from a boy who grew up under the thumb of Vlad Solkov. Lev and Leo might have been raised in a large mansion, but it was just as much a prison as this orphanage was.

I turned when Sister Ionna walked back through the door, handing me a plain black dress, socks and slippers, while Lev was given black slacks and a black button, likely from one of the Fathers. "I don't want any of the children to see you," she said while staring at us. "Is there someone I should be calling?"

Lev shook his head, "I have a phone, sister, but thank you." This seemed to appease her, and she walked back out the door.

"Oh, I need to ask her something." Before Lev tried to stop me, I said, "I'll only be a moment."

I quickly left the office, catching Sister Ionna before she reached the great hall. She had stepped off to the side near a sitting area, likely knowing I'd want to speak with her. She'd always had a sixth sense that made me shiver.

"Thank you, Sister, for giving us a warm place to wait. I never thought I'd see the inside of this place ever again."

Her cold eyes appraised me. "Bringing back warm and cosy memories, is it?"

I bit my tongue, knowing she was trying to get a rise out of me, just like when I was a girl.

"Only the memories of the church's charity, Sister Ionna."

Her brow raised again, the only part of her face that expressed any emotions. She was quiet before clasping her hands. "We did not know about your family, Anastasia," she said pointedly. "And I was to give me condolences. The Romanovs were always a friend to the church."

Until it came time to accept Solkov's money.

I forced myself to smile. "A past I can not remember has changed my future. I never thought I'd be a wife to a br-."

She raised her bony finger. "Your husband is a businessman and benefactor of the church. That is all."

That's right because we never actually said *Bratva* here within these hallowed halls.

"Right, but I was hoping to ask one more favour of you, Sister. A favour for a Saint Basil's orphan."

Her lips twitched, but she nodded her head for me to continue.

"I need to speak with Father Grigori Rasputin."

Leo

I loved her, and I might never get to hear her say it back.

Who am I kidding? Why would she? What indication have I ever given her that she mattered more to me than her name on paper? In what world am I deserving of her love?

These are the questions I ask myself while tied to a broken chair, deep below the floors of Chateau Barone, with a prayer on my lips that Ana and Lev were far, far away.

"She was a quality counterfeit," Alexei said condescendingly. "Better than anything I could have come up with. Where did you get her?"

I was silent, staring straight ahead while blood ran down my neck. The bullet wound on my cheek had stopped bleeding, but my now broken nose was a mess I don't think even the best plastic surgeon could fix. I had been surrounded only seconds after Ana and my brother had left me in that hall, beaten to the ground by nearly a dozen men in blood-stained coats.

"You know, I remember you from when we were children." Alexei sat back against the cellar wall, sleeves rolled up to his elbows while a scalpel was twisted between his fingers. "You were always so quiet, but I was terrified of you," a chuckle escaped his lips. "Now look at us. No longer children."

I shook my head, staring off to the other side of the room and wondering where the fuck my men were. There should have been at least twenty men outside with automatic weapons, and yet I sit here without another sound to be heard in the house.

"You were going to be a big deal, marrying Olga and holding the D.C. seat. Why wasn't that enough for old Vladimir? The capital whores were getting old, so he decided to try New York on for size?"

When I refused to look at him, he lurched off the wall, sticking the blade into my right shoulder and slowly pressing it in. Savouring the way the veins in my neck bulged against the pain. "Look at me, you fucking pig," he snarled.

"No." I grit out through a clenched jaw.

He sat back a little, surprised that I had actually spoken. "No? Am I not worthy of your gaze, *King of New York*?"

I turned my head and spit blood onto the floor near his feet. "I don't wish to see her eyes staring at me with so much hate."

He was silent, but the scalpel raised under my chin until I had to focus on a point above his head to avoid his gaze. "Who's eyes?"

A small smile tugged at my lips. "You know, she looks the most like your mother. Alexandra had the most beautiful blue eyes."

The blade was tugged away as if I could have turned it back on him. Alexei's feet slid across the floor until he knelt on one knee and looked up at me. His blonde hair was cut short, tattoos kissing the back of his neck like many bratva boys. "Ana died protecting me. I saw her body."

I shook my head once. "Ana was sent to Saint Basil's while you were taken out of the city. Father Grigori was supposed to get you both out."

He laughed, "Are you trying to tell me that you aided my escape? The great prince of the Solkov bratva betrayed his *papa* to help two young orphans? Orphaned by *your* father?"

I bit down on my tongue hard, not saying another word before his fists connected with the side of my jaw, and the world turned sideways. He'd hit me so hard that the chair legs broke below me, and my head connected with the cold stone floor of the cellar with a heavy smack.

My right ear rang out, vision blurry before I felt the white hold, slicing pain of the scalpel across my left cheek.

"Argh," I ground out through my teeth. I wouldn't give the kid satisfaction.

Alexei bent down so he was forcing his face into mine, and my vision blurred against images of crystal blue eyes that lit up at the sight of an old book. I would think of those eyes, and the pain would be over soon.

"There will be a special seat in hell for you, Leonid Solkov. It'll be a large table full of men like our fathers before us. I'm sure I'll meet you down there, but you'll be there first to welcome me."

I smiled, swallowing past the clumps of blood that threatened to choke me. "But it will never be you who sits on the throne of New York. Even if I'm dead, my legacy will pass to my brother - and your seat - that will be given to whoever your widowed sister decides to marry after me."

This time, Alexei chuckled, and I could hear him sitting back, so he was on the floor near me. "You think I would allow that girl to live after this? You have everyone convinced she's Anastasia. You've given a poor little girl too much power, and her death will be on your hands. Just as the real Anastasia is." I heard him pushing away from me, and I winced against the concrete floor.

"Alexei, she's real. It's not too late for you to have your sister back."

His cold hand shot out and wrapped around my cheek, thumbing digging into the bullet wound and allowing for fresh blood to flow down my skin. "Where is your honour, Leonid? Where was your outrage when Olga was gunned down in her own home? Yet you continue to try and torture me, even with your dying breath, spreading lies."

He pushed off of me, and I heard his footsteps retreating, my body convulsing while still tied to the fucking chair. "Don't hurt her, Alexei. Alexie," I shouted, but no one responded. "Alexie!"

Ana

The auditorium had felt so much more imposing when I was a child, crafted out of the cheap seats and dark red curtains that always carried a slight scent of mould and desperation. I'd bled countless times on that stage, but I'd never allowed myself to cry.

The nuns despised tears.

The back of Father Grigori's head was a dark spot against the Christmas concert's bright lights, almost illuminating a bow of pale yellow around his head like an angel's halo.

The irony.

I moved into the seats behind him, sitting down and casting my eyes over the five sugar plum faeries that twirled around on well-worn point shoes. Watching them made my legs ache in the most beautiful and painful way. I loved ballet as a girl, even though it was used to control the masses within the orphanage. Ballet was a duty, not a privilege. If you were not fit enough to dance on that stage, you were cast to the backrooms, where you sewed clothing and walked away with more needle punctures than you could count.

I was never so unlucky.

As a child, my quiet but spiteful demeanour meant that the nuns kept a close eye on me. I was always alone, rushing through chores to be back on that stage with my toes bleeding through my pale pink shoes.

The nuns would have used the *Needle Room*, as the girls called it, as punishment if I wasn't so exceptional on stage.

"Talent is sometimes given to those who do not deserve it," Sister Ionna had said many times as I pranced past her to the practice room. It also made me a target for the other girls, being centre stage at every dance, even though no one came to see our shows.

Many of those girls were sent to the *Needle Room*, where clothes pins would be left open in my dresses, and my point shoes would be beaten down. I hid my shoes after a while because one could live with a few pokes, but breaking an ankle due to the wrong shoes would not be my fate. As I got older, I mainly stuck to myself, sleeping in the corners away from others and staying quiet until I could escape to the stage.

Leaving this place was bitter-sweet because it meant I was allowed to make my own decisions, but I was also giving up my only pleasure in life. I haven't danced since I left Saint Basil's.

"Reminiscing, *svoyenravnyy rebenok?*" Father Grigori's voice was quiet in the room.

Of course, he'd known it was me; the man had a devilish sixth sense that was not a God-given gift. His haunting blue eyes stared daggers through me as a child, always watching. Now I know it's because he is interested in the long-lost Romanov princess.

"You came to every one of my Christmas concerts," I said while leaning back in the creaking seat. I was still shivering as I hadn't returned to change my clothes, so the wet fabric clung to my small frame. "Every year, you would single me out, and I had no idea why."

The back of his head tilted, but his gaze was still focused on the young girls who danced their hearts out on stage. "You were an exceptional student of the arts, Anastasia."

I let a grin slip onto my lips, though sour. "And I was a Romanov."

Grigorio was quiet for a moment, but then he nodded slowly. "Not in these walls, you weren't. You were never meant to go back to that life."

I moved over a seat, leaning forward to see the side of the Father's face - thin and cast with shadows. "But destiny has a funny way of coming back to us, hm? It seems I was always destined to marry Leo, not Olga. Did you know her, Father?"

Grigori's head turned my way; his clouded eyes looked sombre. "She was a beautiful young girl, but as all your siblings were."

"Alexei's still handsome, Father. I saw him only hours ago."

His eyes widened momentarily before he looked back towards the Nutcracker, watching the Nutcracker soldiers leap across the stage. Tchaikovsky's music fluttered around us as I stared down the man who purposefully kept me from my past. My future.

"What is it you need from me, my child?"

I wanted to wrap my hands around his sallow, thin throat and squeeze until he could see the Lord, but I needed him. "A meeting with Alexei."

"I thought you just saw him?"

I nodded, "And I need a meeting to discuss my husband's business."

The Father's head returned to me again, and his eyes wandered over my frazzled hair and damp clothing. "Leonid was always good at getting himself into precarious situations, even as a young boy."

I nodded. "Two young boys are fighting to be King of the Hill, but one has a gun."

Father Grigori huffed. "I think it is safe to assume that they both have a gun, but in Leo's case, you're the loaded weapon."

I agreed with him. "I need you to vouch for me. Tell Alexei that I am his sister."

Father Grigori stared at me for a moment longer, his eyes focusing on my hair and sliding down my cheek in a way that made me want to retch. Finally, he gave me a small grunt. "I'll call him after the concert."

"I need to see him now."

He sighed, "It will take time to contact him and return to the city."

"Good thing he's at the Barone estate then."

Grigori looked surprised, but then he pursed his lips. "And this is where you saw him?"

I nodded, "And where my husband commanded his brother to carry me away, kicking and screaming."

"Then let us go. I don't wish to see you a widow so soon, Anastasia."

Ana

I'd given Sister Ionna a note to pass off to Lev once we were safely away. I knew he could come running after me, but I was hoping to make it to Alexei before Igor could pick him up. This was between siblings.

The four hours we'd traversed through the woods were twiddled down into a mere twenty minutes, and I'd been able to change into the plain black dress before we left. Father Grigori called while I was changing and told me we were expected soon.

The ride was silent; my face pushed against the cold glass as the dark forest passed us in a blur. I had no idea what I would say to Alexei to change his mind about the brothers, but I had to try. If not for Leo, then for Lev, who'd helped me through a very dark time. For Lev, who just wanted to escape to his piano and be a million miles away but was cursed into the bratva life.

Pulling up to the front of the Barone estate was much different than fleeing through the backdoor. Pulling towards the front gate, two SUVs were blocking the road ahead, and an armed man stepped out to talk with Grigori.

The man was clad in the signature black suit of the bratva, head-shaven and tattoos swirling around his collar. They all appeared like little soldiers, dispensable and indiscernible. *"Otets Grigoriy, mne skazali vas ozhidat'."*

The Father nodded. "And I have a guest."

The soldier's eyes flickered to me, a scowl on his face before he turned and waved to the drivers in the SUVs to move. We were about to pull forward when the man's hand clamped down on the open window. "You'll be checked at the door."

For guns. He didn't need to say it.

The house, if you could call it that, sprawled across acres of snow and had lights lining the long drive. The entire place was lit like a Christmas tree, with spotlights shining down on the circle drive and men walking the grounds. It seems Leo and Lev's rescue mission had everyone on high alert.

The moment we pulled up, there was a man to open my door, stepping aside as I got out of the car and instantly blocking my path. *"Ruki naruzhu."*

I rolled my eyes but stuck out my arms as his hands wrapped around my shoulders and patted me down. When he bent down to wrap his hands around my thighs, a ringed hand settled on his shoulder.

"Now, we can leave a little to the imagination, can't we *principessa?*"

I didn't recognise the man in front of us, but I'd bet everything he was part of the Barone family. His black hair was slicked back, and a devilish smile was splayed across his Mediterranean features. He was handsome but in a dangerous sort of way. Not the jagged edge of black like the Solkov brothers, but like an ember that could burst into flames with the correct change of the wind.

"Enzo Barone," he said before bringing my hand to his lips. His eyes never left mine as he placed a kiss on my cold skin, lingering there while I tried to smile.

"Anastasia Solkov," I replied to him, liking the way it rolled over my tongue.

Enzo's eyes were alight with mischief. "Oh, we know. The woman of the hour and supposed sister to the man who's taken over my home."

His lips curled as he said this, a bit of venom dripping from his tongue.

"And where is Alexei," I asked while my eyes scanned the battalion of men who lined the front steps.

The man looked over his shoulder, then offered me his arm cloaked in an expensive silk suit. "Right this way."

I looked over to Father Grigori, sending him a pleading look as he allowed Enzo to take my arm and walk me through the grand doors of *Chateau* Barone. The Father merely looked at me and then stood by as I was rushed into the house - alone in the hornet's nest once more.

The entry hall of the manor was littered with bullet holes, though the floors had swept away any remaining debris. A faint smell of gunpowder still sat in the air, and many of the men we passed had scratches and blood soaking their colours.

"Your husband is an exceptionally violent man, *principessa*," Enzo said as we walked into a small sitting room. "My Father wants his head, but it seems your brother already owns it."

The room was covered in dark woods, just like the one I'd been held in, with deep blue drapes that screamed old world and stone statues that lined the shelves. The entire manor was a picture of elegance, punctured by my husband's wrath.

My arm tightened in his hold, a cold chill racing my spine. "Is he . . . Is my husband. . ."

Enzo released me before shaking his head, "Not yet, but he will be soon. Don't get me wrong, *principessa*, I admire the man. Leonid Solkov worked closely with my family to try and bring order to the city, but his mess here can not go unpunished."

I backed away from him, anger in my gaze. "He wouldn't have had to make a mess if the Italians had minded their own business. What is really in it for you, working with Alexei? Did he promise a seat at the table? You'd get any city you want in the east once the other vors were gone?"

Enzo's tongue pushed into his cheek before he chuckled. "You have crime in your blood, Anastasia. That much is true."

I straightened my shoulders. "Romanov by birth, and Solkov by marriage. Do you think Alexei can really give you the things you want? Look at your home, Enzo."

The man's eyes glanced around the room that had overturned chairs and holes in the walls. If this was his family home, Alexei had led wolves to his den. The Italians couldn't appreciate that, nor the loss of life on their side. They were dragged into this war and would not get any of the spoils.

"I'll leave you to it, *principessa*," Enzo said before turning for the door and sidestepping a tall blonde caked in dried blood.

"I can not tell if you are exceptionally fearless or half-witted for coming back here when you had made it out. I was surprised to hear Father Grigori's voice but even more shocked to hear you were half an hour away, tucked into the old orphanage Leo dug you out of."

Alexei closed the large door behind him and turned the bolt to lock us both in. I tried to keep myself calm, but my heart was leaping into my throat, making it nearly impossible to form words.

"I want to make a deal."

Alexei smiled wide, his teeth shining in the lamplight as he unbuttoned his ruined sports coat and threw it over the back of a chair. "You can continue."

Arrogant prick.

"I want Leo released and allowed to relocate to another city. He should be able to keep the brotherhood seat that was his by birth, but not from New York."

Alexei's brows raised, his head tilting to the side as he took a seat and motioned for me to as well. "I hope you realise that Leo would never give up this city, just as I won't. He'd rather die."

"We won't give him a choice," I said firmly.

Alexei chuckled, "We?"

"Yes, the last of the Romanovs. This city is ours by blood, but you are entitled to a seat at the table. The sins of the father shouldn't stain the son."

His eyes darkened, and his gaze wandered over me again with hatred. "Why do you keep this up," he asked with a wave. "Every time you open your mouth, I don't know if it will release reason or lies."

How else could I convince him? I didn't have a solid memory to share, so I was entirely at the mercy of his anger. Father Grigori was supposed to be with me to tell Alexei it was the truth!

He shook his hand. "I must admit, though, you look well in the bratva life. What did Leo promise you for your part in all this?"

"My brother's life," I snarled back at him before I could hold my tongue. "I was shown six headless bodies and six matching crimson crosses. The choice was my signature on a marriage contract or your head handed over to the families."

Alexei pursed his lips, but he did not look moved. He leaned back in the leather chair, crossing a leg over his knee and giving me a tight smile. "So why do you risk your life for a man who threatened your *brother*," he emphasised.

"Because I'd never known family, and the thought of losing you when I could save you instead was worth my freedom."

He blinked, running his finger over his knee. "So you are a prisoner in the Solkov home?"

I winced. "That wasn't the right word to use?"

"No?" He stood up quickly and stepped right into my personal space, the smell of blood and whiskey rolling off of him. "So if I could offer you freedom, you wouldn't take it? A new passport and a ticket anywhere you want?"

I swallowed. "My place is with my family, including my husband."

Alexei's face squished in anger, his hands clenching into fists at his sides. This close, I could see the resemblance that he was too furious to admire. Our high cheekbones and almond-shaped eyes were light blue. He even had my same upturned nose.

"Fine, then let's take you to him."

Before I could stop him, Alexei had his fingers wrapped around my upper arm like an iron vice, pulling me through the door and away from the crowd of mafia and bratva men who were guarding the entrance. My eyes met Enzo's from across the room, and he lowered his gaze as my brother forced me down a flight of stairs.

"Where's Father Grigori? He'll tell you that I'm not lying. Alexei?"

The cellar was dark, and the wooden steps creaked under our feet while Alexei yanked me behind him. "Alexei, please." I tried, but when we reached the bottom of the stairs, his arm shoved me forward and onto a damp, cold floor that reached for blood.

It was everywhere, but I couldn't see it. The pool I was kneeling in still felt warm, and my hands shuffled around the shallow puddle until I felt a drenched piece of fabric under my fingers. Then, the light was turned on, and I winced against the sudden intrusion.

"Fitting, isn't it?" Alexei asked. "This is exactly how my family went - broken on the floor of a cellar near the end of December. I do love it when it comes full circle."

I blinked as my vision cleared, and I looked down to see my knees resting in a large pool of crimson that spread across the room - spreading from my husband, who lay dying on the concrete floor.

Ana

"Leo?" My hands shook as they hovered over his crumbled form. "Leo, can you hear me?" He was wearing only a white shirt that was soaked all the way through in blood, his chest exposed to show an array of slash marks and purple ribs.

I swung around to see Alexei sneering down at us. "I told you I would make you a deal. Anything."

He rolled his eyes. "What could you possibly give me that I won't inherit the moment he stops breathing?"

"Levandr is still alive," I grit out. "He'll be the one inheriting New York unless I convince him to hand it over, which he won't do if his brother is dead!"

Leo's body shook as he tried to take a breath, and my fingers gently ran over his forehead, pushing back the hair that often fell into his beautiful dark eyes. I'd never been able to imagine him as powerless because Leonid Solkov radiated authority and might. His body was rigid and sculpted, and I could have withered under his gaze a million times.

The man lying in front of me was not Leonid Solkov, though. The bloodied man at my feet, the one who stayed behind so Lev and I could escape - the man at my feet was my *husband*.

"What I want is the truth of who the fuck you are," Alexei said as he leaned down to look at Leo and me. "Start there, and I might consider giving him a quick death."

Where the fuck was Grigori?

"I went my Anzelina at Saint Basil's, presumed an orphan when I was dropped off at the doors over ten years ago on a New Year's Eve - I was covered in blood with no memories of who I was. I still can't recall someone saying my name or what my mother's perfume smelled like. All I've had was a memory of a red-haired woman and a gold chain she wore."

Alexei's face screwed up again before he grabbed my neck, bringing me closer to him. "You've rehearsed that well. Tell me. Who. You. Are."

My fingers clawed at his hand as the air was tugged from my lungs, Leo stirring at our feet. "Anastasia Solkov, daughter of Nicholas Romanov and - Argh!"

I was yanked over Leo's body, my feet dragging across the damp floor until he threw me into the corner, where my head bashed into the cellar floor. I didn't have a second to breathe before my brother's hand was back around my throat, pushing me into the cement while he raged above me.

"You fucking bitch, I'll get it out of you one way or another." He growled down at me, his body pinning me in place while I kicked and thrashed below him. His thighs were on either side of me, caging me.

"P-p-please, Alexie," I sputtered. His other hand came up to grab a fist full of my hair, yanking my neck to the side.

"You do look so much like her," he said through exposed teeth. His lips were curled back, his face lined in cold rage. "Maybe I'll keep you around." Alexei's eyes suddenly went cold, all emotion draining from them as his fingers started to curl through my hair.

I still couldn't speak with his hand around my neck, but my eyes widened as he leaned forward and smashed his lips into mine. I tried screaming, but his teeth dug into my lips, and I could taste blood on my tongue. His hold on me was unbreakable, furious and cold as I tried to push him away.

When he pulled back, I gasped as crimson lined his lips. He smiled, releasing my hair to wipe a thumb across the blood. "Whoever you are, I'm not letting you -."

Alexei was cut off by a circle of rope wrapping around his neck, tugging him off of me as his eyes opened in shock. He was pulled back onto the attacker, noose cutting into the skin of his neck as he kicked out.

"Leo!" I screamed as my husband used all of his remaining energy to strangle my brother, both of their body squirming on the floor. I watched Alexei's eyes blown wide in hatred, staring into my own even though Leo was taking his breath away. Cutting off his airways with the same rope he used to bind him.

"You're killing him," I cried as I watched Alexei's feet scramble below him. The rope was digging so hard into his skin that it started to bleed, flesh taring under the power of Leonid, even on death's door.

Do I stop him? Alexei didn't believe me, and he was going to . . .

The man under that rope was not the blonde-haired boy that I'd seen in those photos or the one whose body I'd protected in the cellar of our family estate.

I crawled closer, tears running down my face as I sobbed. "I'm so sorry, Alexei. I'm so sorry I couldn't protect you."

His lips were curled back in a snarl, his eyes baring into mine as his motions became jerky. Alexei's eyes started drooping, legs going still as his chest heaved for air he would never get.

When he went utterly still, eyes still blown open in a fury, I fell forward until my head was against his chest, and I wept. I screamed into him, cursing him for being unable to set his hatred aside and for ruining any chance we both had at freedom. At peace.

I felt a hand clasp onto mine, and I gasped when the familiar cold touch of Leo's ring made me remember that he was still bleeding out. I pulled Alexei's body off of him, my knees trembling as I crumbled next to my husband, who was gurgling.

"Leo," I sobbed. "You fucking idiot! You should have come with us," I said while my hands roamed his body for injuries. "I have to get you out of here. You need a doctor."

He shook his head, eyes staring into mine as his lips quivered. I'd looked into his eyes numerous times, wanting to drown in the deep depths of him. To be encompassed and consumed by him, even though he promised only darkness.

Leo smiled at me through the pain. *"We are asleep until we fall in love. Thank you for waking me up, Ana."*

I cried, holding his head in my hands. "How dare you quote Tolstoy to me in a time like this," I said as his eyes started to flutter. My body went cold with panic, my hands moving to his cheeks. "No, Leo. You have to stay awake. I'm getting you out of here."

He merely smiled at me again, his lips parted with a ragged breath. "Take care of my brother, Ana. You're going to need each other. Take care of him."

I shook my head. "No, no, we're going to see him again. You're going to see him again. Leo?" I looked down at him, his face calm as he stared back at me. Unblinking.

"Leo!" My heart leapt into my chest, tears spilling over onto his bloodied chest as I sobbed in the damp cellar that was now a crypt to my brother and husband. Gone within minutes of one another. I rocked back and forth, his head held tight against my chest as I screamed, and screamed, and screamed.

Epilogue

The snow had finally melted in the streets of New York, and the rainy season meant that everywhere you looked, there were colourful umbrellas and children splashing in dirty water that covered the sidewalks as they laughed and screamed.

My eyes roamed over the inhabitants of Cobble Hill, all none the wiser to the horrors that had befallen the great house of Solkov or the change their city was sure to see in the coming years as a new vor took control.

The moving truck pulled away from our door, carrying away years of history to a new home far away from this cursed city. When I walked back through the doors, Igor nodded as I passed and gave me a warm smile. He would be coming with us and a few others who had no interest in staying behind for a city that never loved them.

They had all been orphans from Saint Basil's.

"Our flight leaves in an hour, Ana!" Lev screamed from the office, his voice echoing in the empty house.

I smiled, walking around the corner and leaning into the door frame as Lev scurried around the near-empty room, plucking a picture frame from the wall and tucking it into a leather bag. I knocked, and he spun around to greet me with wide eyes. "Are you ready? This is the last flight to London today, and I want to be buried in my headphones before it takes off.

I chuckled and rolled my eyes. "The truck is already gone, taking it to the docks. Getting to London will take a week, so I hope you packed enough underwear."

He snorted, walking towards me and placing a small kiss on my forehead. "I'm pretty sure you packed all of the bags, so I guess we'll find out."

Lev ducked past me into the hall, and I let my eyes wander over the room that had once been Leo's. My chest felt like it was splitting in two when I heard his name, but it was getting easier. I had to be strong for Lev.

Enzo had found me in the basement beside the two men and declared that the blood feud was over. The man who he was working with was dead, and so was the one who attacked his home and Antonio - a cousin of Enzo's that my husband had interrogated for my location. Leo's backup had been stopped in New York, a pile-up on the Hudson Parkway that was the cause of black ice on the bridge.

Watching Lev's cold gaze follow his brother's body into the SUV was almost harder than witnessing Leo's death. I at least got to say goodbye. After a week-long tirade of pulling Lev from the bathroom floor, covered in his own puke and tears, he woke up one morning, flushed everything he had down the toilet and called a doctor.

He was too much of a target for rehab, and so was I, so we started an at-home treatment for three months while Igor helped establish an exchange of power from the Solkovs to the Ivanov family.

Lev and I were 42 days sober today.

I kept my promise and stayed through all the bad days to be here for Lev. He tried to be strong but was far more fragile than he wanted anyone to know. There were nights when he'd crawl into my bed and just let me hold him. I don't think he could recall a time when he'd just been held - loved.

The new vor of New York, Dmitri Ivanov, was the only child of a

Russian migrant who landed in Boston when he was only ten, and he's been a branch of a few larger families for years. He promised to maintain donations to the orphanage and protection for any Solkov who wished to return to the city, and all of the Solkov men could either be dissolved into his bratva or leave the life of crime behind without fear. Many still chose to stay.

Giving up the seat was not a hard decision for Levandr to make regarding the bratva because we both knew what Leo would have wanted. He died so we could have a second chance, and that meant living the life we were supposed to have. The only one that destiny tried to rob us of. The Solkov estate was worth millions, and it was more than enough for both of us to live on for many lifetimes.

The symbolic keys to the kingdom were handed off a week ago with a grand party surrounded by the brotherhood, all of whom told me they would be interested in a marriage contract.

I don't believe I would ever marry again, though. I would remain Mrs.Solkov for the rest of my days and wear Leo's ring.

My seat was also transferred to Lev when Leo died, the Russian brotherhood being strong in their patriarchal ties. That seat was not so quickly filled, but it wasn't New York, so Lev wiped his hands off it and signed it over to the brotherhood.

April would be even rainier in London, but it would give us enough time to settle into our new flat above a small dance studio. I was too out of practice to pursue ballet myself, but the passion was still alive. It would be a place for Lev and I to start over, feed our love for music and forget about all the horrors our lives had dealt us.

I looked at the dark room, my finger rolling over the ring that now sat like a heavy stone on my left hand. When I came home after that terrible night, I shut myself in the library and nearly drank myself to death. I'd swept books from their shelves, thrown bottles into the fire, and collapsed in tears. After waking up covered in sweat, I saw the still unopened box that contained my engagement ring. My hands shook while opening and finding the perfect jewel inside, nestled onto a gold band.

"It'd been our mother's," Lev told me after seeing it on my hand. His eyes had settled on it for a while before a small smile tugged at the corners of his mouth. *"Maybe my brother had a heart after all."*

I closed the door, wincing as the bolt clicked into place before joining the men at the door.

"No, you're not seated right next to us. Why does that matter?" Leo asked while pulling a raincoat from his suitcase. "It's first-class; only two seats are together. You're with Mikhail. I don't care if he snores; wear headphones."

I rolled my eyes as Ignore straightened the moment I walked into the room, still very much calling me *Ma'am* and *Mrs. Solkov* whenever he had the chance. It hurt a little each time I heard *Mrs* these days, especially when it was meant with respect and not a pitying look from a brotherhood member.

"Is he bothering you, Igor?"

The large man blushed, pulling back his shoulders. "No, ma'am."

Lev and Igor continued to bicker as we headed towards the airport, my head leaning against the glass as the only city I've ever known passed by me. I didn't know if I'd ever return to New York because the day I did would have to mean that I was healed.

Whole again.

But I didn't think I could ever stitch back the tares left by Leonid or the bleeding gash left by a brother I failed to save. I didn't talk about Alexei unless it came to business, and when the DNA test came back positive, all of his accounts were transferred to me as his only living relative. Now, indeed, the last Romanov.

It was hard because both of the damaged little boys died on the hill they tried so desperately to conquer. Lev lost a brother, and so did I.

The look of silent pain still flashed in his eyes when he heard Alexei's name, and I couldn't blame him. Leo's body was shredded to pieces in that basement, and the coroner said it was a miracle he was able to take Alexei with him.

If I could go back, I ask myself what I would have done differently. For a while, I told myself I wouldn't have tried to reason with Alexei because he was too far gone. Mad, out of his mind with a lust for revenge that I would never have been able to stop. He would have killed me and then given up his pursuit of New York.

But he was wrong about Leo because the eldest Solkov brother didn't die for his throne. He died for me.

Odysseus died so his darling witch could escape the island they'd both been imprisoned on.

"Thank you for waking me up, Leonid."

Also by Ariella Isabella

THE BLOOD IS LIFE
Part One : A Stranger Called Conrad
Part Two : A Creature Called Grace (Spring 2024)
*This series will be long, and span across multiple novellas before they
are put into one novel*
KINGS OF NEW YORK (MAFIA & BRATVA ROMANCE)
Things I Almost Remember : A Bratva Romance
GODS FROM THE OBLIVION
A Secret Shared with Death (April 9th, 2024)
A Secret Shared with Sirens (TBA)
A Secret Shared with Darkness (TBA)

Acknowledgments

First of all, this was the most challenging story I have ever written, and I don't know the next time I'll try my hand at contemporary dark fiction. My soul hurt when I couldn't make Leo or Lev a shadow daddy. I pushed through this novel because, well, I had published the pre-sale, so I had to, but also because I wanted to write something that hurt, where the dark MMC didn't get his happy ending even though the FMC was okay in the end.

I want to thank my work-wife, Tayla, for constantly pushing me through things, even from the other side of the world. Your constant reassurance and presence have been a Godsend, and I don't know where I would be without you! (I promise we will meet in Scotland someday and leave our muggle lives behind.)

Nick, my life partner and shoulder to cry on, I'm sorry I put you through the pressure of me writing yet another story that's not on my calendar. I'll try my best next year, but I make no promises.

To my Street Team: Nathalie, Courtney C, Tayla, Alexa, Brianna, Zoe T, Gabrielle P, Emma M, Rebecca S, Molly, Devon U, Joana, Shannon I, Gabriela, Chelsea, Megan, Dakota, Kaylee, Alex & Jennifer R, this was a last-minute drop. I've lived in a hole for the last three months, but 2024 will be my year! I have to get this story out, and everything else is . . . well, it's still an uphill battle, but at least I have on the proper shoes now.

And finally, to all my author friends who have supported me on my journey. Y'all are the best coworkers a gal could ask for.

Keeping up with Ariella

If you'd like to stay up to date on everything going on all the crazy manuscripts I have planned, follow my socials.

Website:

https://www.ariellaisabella.com/

Facebook :

Ariella's Darklings : A Dark Fantasy Reader Group

Instagram:

@author.ariella

Amazon:

https://www.amazon.com/stores/Ariella-Isabella/author/B0CCLN4
ZM7?ref=ap_rdr&store_ref=ap_rdr&isDramIntegrated=true&shoppi
ngPortalEnabled=true

Goodreads:

https://www.goodreads.com/author/show/37056134.Ariella_Isabella

About Ariella

Living with my partner and an array of animals in New Hampshire, I enjoy traveling the world and writing stories that make your heart hurt and question your morals. I was influenced by the rise of Anne Rice, dark southern Gothics, and epic fantasies by Carissa Broadbent. I spend far too much of my time reading Dramione fan fiction and thinking of new ways to break hearts.